OPERATION

Eiffel TOWER

OPERATION
Eiffel
TOWER

ELEN CALDECOTT

BLOOMSBURY
LONDON NEW DELHI NEW YORK SYDNEY

Bloomsbury Publishing, London, New Delhi, New York and Sydney

First published in Great Britain in July 2011 by Bloomsbury Publishing Plc
50 Bedford Square, London WC1B 3DP

A CIP catalogue record for this book is available from the British Library

ISBN 978 1 4088 0573 2

Typeset by Hewer Text UK Ltd, Edinburgh
Printed and bound in Great Britain by CPI Group (UK) Ltd, Croydon CR0 4YY

7 9 10 8

www.bloomsbury.com

To my friends at the Watershed

CHAPTER 1

The ball flew clean over the Atlantic Ocean and dropped – *plop* – into the hole by the Statue of Liberty's size-twelve feet.

'A hole-in-one!' Jack cried. 'Hole-in-one, hole-in-one, hole-in-one!' He lifted the club and twirled it as though he were leading a brass band down the High Street. 'Did you see that?' he asked.

Lauren looked up from her magazine. 'Nope,' she grinned. 'I wasn't watching. You'll have to do it again.'

'I want a go of the stick,' Ruby said.

'It's called a club,' Jack said.

'I want a go of the club,' Ruby said. There was a determined crease between her eyebrows. Sometimes Ruby looked just like Mum.

'Let her have a go,' Lauren said, and looked back at *Teen Thing*.

1

'I was going to. I just wanted her to learn the right name, that's all. Come on, Ruby, it's a par-three hole. That means you should be able to get it in three hits. Or, if you're a genius like me, you might do it in one.'

Jack handed the club over to Ruby. He fished the ball out of the hole and wiped it on his jeans; it left a green slug-trail on his leg. *Yuck!* In winter, it would be his job to scrub all the crud out of the holes. And glue down curling greens. And nail up wobbly fences. And a hundred and one other odd jobs that needed doing once all the visitors went home. But now it was summer and he was allowed to play for free at William's World of Wonders Golf Tour.

Jack smiled a secret smile.

A hole-in-one.

'My go, my go,' Ruby said.

'I know. Hold your horses.'

He teed up the ball, balancing it on its plastic holder. It was all set for Ruby to swing. The club was too big for her; it waved from side to side, like jelly in a high wind. She tried to steady herself, then gave the ball a good hard shove towards the Statue of Liberty. It rolled forward along the causeway to the island, then veered left and dropped, with a splash, into the miniature Atlantic Ocean, where it bobbed gently up and down as though it were enjoying the swim.

'Hey!' Ruby yelled indignantly. 'It went in the water.'

Jack couldn't help himself – he laughed. Lauren looked up and even she smiled.

'You want a go?' Jack asked her.

Lauren sucked her teeth in a way that meant, 'I'd rather roll in horse poo than play adventure golf,' and lifted *Teen Thing* in front of her face.

Last year she would have played. Last summer, when Paul was still around and it was his job to look after them and Lauren wasn't quite so grown-up, then she would have taken a turn.

Jack reached into the miniature ocean and grabbed the ball. He gave it a few shakes to get rid of some of the water, then put it back on the causeway.

'Have another go,' he said to Ruby.

She tried again. This time the ball rolled in a straight line towards Ellis Island, but slowed too soon, as though its batteries had run down.

'You do it,' Ruby said, handing him the club. 'Make it go in the hole.'

'OK, if you're sure. He held the club with a firm grip but with loose wrists, just like Dad had taught him. Then he gave the ball a gentle tap. It rolled steadily up the slope towards the three-metre-high statue and dropped neatly into the hole with a soft puttering sound.

Ruby clapped her hands together, her dark curls bouncing. 'I got it in the hole!' she yelled.

'Did you?' Jack asked.

'Yes. If I hadn't got it to there,' Ruby pointed to Ellis Island, 'then you wouldn't have got it in like that.'

'I see.' Jack grinned. 'Do you want to do a harder one, then? The Eiffel Tower is tricky.'

'We need to get back,' Lauren said. 'Mum will be wondering where we've got to.'

Jack sighed.

'One more go?' Ruby asked hopefully.

Lauren paused, then shook her head. 'No.'

Jack retrieved the ball. He squeezed it in his palm. He liked the feel of its hard dimpled shell. He threw it up and caught it.

'Jack,' Lauren said, 'come on.' She got up off the bench and closed her magazine. The girl on the cover had a wide lipstick smile, as though nothing bad could ever happen in the world.

Jack nodded slowly. Lauren was right – it was time to go back. He just wished they didn't have to.

Near the exit, William, owner of William's World of Wonders, sat in his booth. Jack handed back the club and dropped the ball into a glass dish on the counter top. 'See you tomorrow,' he said.

'Jack.' William nodded curtly. 'Something's up with the Niagara pump. It's more of a Stumble than a Falls today. Come and give us a hand in the morning.'

'OK.'

The baking-hot pavement was crowded with tourists, toddlers with buckets and spades, kids with bodyboards. A horse and carriage trotted past carrying a dark-haired woman and a tattooed man towards the prom. Near the beach steps a busker played Beatles songs.

Jack and Ruby weaved their way around holdalls and windbreaks, trying to keep up with Lauren.

But Lauren kept her head down and walked fast.

Ruby's steps slowed. 'Ja-ack,' she said, almost singing his name.

Jack sighed as Lauren disappeared completely from view.

Ruby stopped dead outside the amusement arcade. 'Ja-ack, can I have twenty pence?'

'I haven't got twenty pence,' he said.

'Yes you have. This morning you gave Mrs Khalid a pound when you bought a comic and she gave you fifty pence change. Two twenties and a ten.'

'When did you get so good at maths?'

'Pwease can I? Pwetty pwease with bells on?'

Jack grinned. 'Don't put on a baby voice. It won't work with me.' Then he handed over twenty pence.

Ruby rested her hands on the grab-a-bear machine, looking in. It was a teddy bear explosion inside – bear faces, bear arms, bear legs and bear bums all pushed up against the glass. Jack grinned. Above the hundreds of bears a mechanical arm hung down, its three claws closed in a trap.

'I want that one,' Ruby said, pointing to a pink smiley bear and pushing Jack's coin into the slot.

The mechanical arm whirred into action as Ruby pressed the controls. It juddered one way, then the other. Finally it came down, claws open, and snatched.

At thin air.

The claws came back up empty. *For a change.*

'Oh!' Ruby said.

'Never mind,' Jack said. 'There's always tomorrow.'

They moved away from the arcade. Ruby scuffed her feet against the pavement.

When they got to the launderette, Lauren was standing outside. Jack could see Mum inside, talking to Auntie Joyce. Billy was in his pushchair by Mum's side. He was asleep, cuddling Teddy Volvo. Mum whipped off her tabard and handed it to Auntie Joyce. That meant her shift was officially over. She smiled and waved at Jack and Ruby.

Now they could all go home.

Jack felt his heart sink.

CHAPTER 2

As soon as they were home, Jack ran up to his room and closed the door. Whatever they were doing down-stairs, he didn't care. In the room next door, Lauren had turned her music up loud; she was keeping out of the way too. Jack switched on his computer. An email from Paul. Jack let himself smile.

To: jack.dempsey23@hotmail.co.uk
From: fulldinnerjacket@gmail.com
Subject: News for my Lil' Crew

Hey Jack,

Are you all missing me? Or is Lauren stepping up OK? I miss you all, little man. No one here will listen to my jokes like you do. Here's a new one for you:

Knock knock.

Who's there?

Soldier.

Soldier who?

Soldier granny on eBay!

LOL! I'd better be careful not to split your sides with these instant classics.

But I guess you really want to know about how awful everything is and how hard they make us work. Well, let me tell you. This morning I ran **thirty miles** carrying **forty kilos** in my rucksack. Don't you believe me? You're right not to. It was **fifty miles** with **sixty kilos** on my back. Still think I'm lying? You're right. It was **a hundred miles** with a **small elephant** on my back.

You don't believe me, do you? Well, you were always good at reading my poker face. Let's just say that the lectures in week one of training were much easier than the exercises in week two.

My feet are ragged. Seriously gross. They're all lumpy and flakey like Cornflake cakes. Yum. I'd send you a picture, but I don't want to give you nightmares.

God bless, little bro. Say hello to your mum and dad, Ruby and Billy. And tell Lauren from me to turn her music down.

Paul (Private Grant these days!)

Jack smiled. Even though Paul was a long way away, it felt as though he was close by. He'd print out the email to show to Auntie Joyce.

Jack banged on the wall that separated his room from Lauren and Ruby's. 'Paul says turn your music down.' Not that Lauren would be able to hear. The music stayed loud.

'She's in a world of her own. Well, a world of Black Eyed Peas's own, anyway.' Dad's voice came from the doorway.

Jack turned. Dad stood leaning up against the door-post. He was still in his work clothes and Jack could see little flakes of plaster in his hair. He must have been doing someone's ceiling. He looked tired, but he was smiling.

'Is that an email from Paul?' he asked.

'Yes. He sent a joke. He sounds OK.'

Dad nodded. 'Don't worry about him. He's safe as houses in Yorkshire. It'll be a long time before he sees any action. I came to see if you want some food. I'm making a sandwich.'

Jack looked down at his hands. If he went downstairs with Dad, he'd have to sit at the kitchen table, watching Mum and Dad not looking at each other. He'd have to tell Paul's new joke into the silence, or pretend to laugh about Ruby not grabbing a bear again, or pretend to

9

moan about how Lauren wouldn't play any more. He sighed. 'It's all right, thanks. I'm not hungry.'

'I'm making your favourite,' Dad said. 'Cheese and tiny-weeny-chunk pickle, cut so small it looks more like gravy.'

'No, I'm OK.'

Dad frowned. 'Oh well, if you're sure.' Then he was gone.

Half an hour later Jack heard shouts from down-stairs, then something smashed – a plate or a cup probably. Then the front door slammed and there was silence.

It was nearly dark when the front door opened again. Dad had come back. Jack was still in his room, chewing the end of a sausage roll. He turned the volume up on his computer game.

Bang, bang, bang! He shot at the shaking zombie figures that lurched towards him. Their heads lolled above their dead shoulders, but they still kept coming. He slotted in another round of ammunition and fired again.

Mum was downstairs in the hallway. Jack heard her say something. He couldn't make out the words, but he could hear that she was still angry. Dad snapped back. They both moved into the kitchen, below Jack's room.

Bang!

A palm slammed on the kitchen table.

Jack's bedroom door was ajar. When twilight faded to darkness outside he didn't turn on his lamp but let light spill in from the landing. From outside it made the room look empty. But tonight he preferred darkness. He paused the game and got up to close the door.

There was someone outside his bedroom: Ruby. She was sitting at the top of the stairs with her chin resting on her knees, her nightie pulled down low over her shins. Jack could see the bumps of her spine pushing against the cloth. She sat still, listening to the noises from downstairs.

'Hey,' Jack whispered.

Ruby looked round. She didn't answer.

'What are you doing?' Jack asked.

'Shh,' Ruby whispered. 'I can't hear.'

'You don't want to,' Jack said. 'Come in here.'

Ruby sighed and stood up. She came into his room and sat down on his bed. She switched on his bedside light.

On the computer screen, the zombies growled and bobbed up and down in the weird way that they did when they were on pause. Like they were happy to wait for ever for a chance to get to their prey.

Jack pushed his door closed and sat back down on his chair.

'You should be in bed,' he said.

'So should you,' Ruby said. 'And Lauren.'

Jack nodded. He noticed that Ruby didn't have any slippers on and her feet had a cold, blueish tinge.

'You can get under the duvet if you want,' he said.

'OK.' Ruby climbed into Jack's bed and pulled the covers up to her chin. She slipped her thumb into her mouth – something she would never, ever do in the daytime. She watched him, saying nothing. Her eyes were wide and glassy. Tomorrow, Jack knew, they would have dark circles under them.

'What do you call a soldier crossed with a fish?' Jack asked.

Ruby shrugged.

'Sturgeon Major.'

She smiled weakly.

Jack turned back to the game. The shots on the screen drowned out the shouts from downstairs. More or less.

'Jack?' she whispered.

'Hmm?'

'Why are they fighting?'

'Well, they're zombies. They're not just going to let me shoot them without a fight.'

'Not them. I mean Mum and Dad.'

Jack's thumb pushed down on the shoot button again and again. He had known what she meant really. 'I don't know,' he said finally. 'Usual stuff: work, money, which one of them was supposed to buy milk.'

'Are they fighting because of us?' Ruby asked.

'No. Not us. Don't worry.'

Ruby jammed her thumb back into her mouth and stroked her nose with her index finger. 'Is it because there are lots of us?' she mumbled.

'We didn't ask to be born, did we?' Jack said. It was something he'd heard Lauren say quite often and it made sense to him.

The kitchen door slammed and there were quick footsteps coming up the stairs.

Jack heard Mum outside his door. 'Jack, turn that game off. You'll keep everyone awake.' Then she went into her room.

Jack scowled at his closed door, but he turned down the volume. 'You should go back to your own bed now,' he told Ruby.

Ruby sighed and pushed back the duvet. 'I don't like sharing with Lauren. I want to share with you.'

'Well, you can't. Billy will be coming in here soon. Mum said. He's too big for their room now. What's wrong with Lauren, anyway?'

Ruby pulled a face. Jack had to laugh; Ruby had caught Lauren's bored, disgusted look exactly.

'She loves you really,' Jack said. He ruffled Ruby's curls. She glared at him and pulled away.

'Don't!'

'Go on,' Jack smiled. 'Get out of here, go get some beauty sleep. You need it.'

Ruby stuck out her tongue and gave Jack a quick hug. Then she was gone.

CHAPTER 3

Jack could smell the soapy, sudsy air as he walked down the street; the door to the launderette was propped open. It was stronger than the smell of car exhausts or hot tarmac; it was even stronger than the smell of his own T-shirt, which was splashed with gunk from the Niagara Falls pump motor. *Stinky.*

But at least he and William had got the Falls working again.

'Hello, everyone!' Jack grinned as he walked in the door.

Lauren was sitting on top of one of the big industrial dryers like a cat curled at a hearth, *Teen Thing* open beside her. Ruby and Billy were messing about with toy bricks on the floor. Mum stood behind the counter, sorting out piles of change from the machines.

'Oh, Jack! What happened to your clothes?' Mum asked.

'It was a global catastrophe. Niagara Falls dried up. It would have changed the whole climate of North America and left millions of people homeless and starving if I hadn't fixed it,' Jack said.

'I see,' Mum said, the corners of her mouth twitching as she tried not to smile. 'Well, I hope it doesn't stain, that's all I can say.'

Jack joined Mum behind the counter and helped her sort out the ten and twenty pences into little towers of pounds.

'Hello, angels!' Auntie Joyce stood in the doorway. 'It's hotter than Kingston out there. Jack, be a good boy and get me drink of water.' She dabbed her forehead with a hanky. In her other hand she held a piece of paper. She came in out of the sun and dropped on to the wooden chair by the counter. Jack nipped into the tiny kitchen out the back and filled a glass.

'You complain about the heat every summer.' Mum smiled at Auntie Joyce. 'You should move to Iceland.'

Auntie Joyce laughed. 'Just think what I'd be like if my mum had stayed in Jamaica. I'd be a grumpy old woman trying to stay in the shade all day!' She finished the water and handed the glass back to Jack.

Auntie Joyce wasn't their real aunt, but she had known them for so long that she nearly was.

'Joyce, you're early,' Mum said, looking at the clock.

'That's because I've got something to show you. Look.' She waved the paper. Jack leaned forward. It was a letter, in Paul's handwriting.

'You should get email,' Jack said.

Auntie Joyce sucked her teeth dismissively. 'Ain't nothing like a letter, is it? I couldn't carry a computer in to show you all!'

'How is he? Is he OK? What does he say?' Mum asked.

Auntie Joyce grinned. 'Listen. I'll read it to you.

' "Dear Mum and Everyone –"

I think he means you lot.

"Private Grant reporting for duty! First off, everything's good, it's all good. Catterick is a lot of fun – it's full of people learning how to be soldiers. The guys in my platoon are all sound. They come from all over: Blackpool, Liverpool, Cumbria. But even some from other countries: Jamaica, South Africa. I asked some of the Jamaican guys if they knew Grandpa, but they didn't. I am sharing sleeping quarters with 11 men – the snoring sounds like we are already at war!

They weren't kidding in the recruitment office when they said it was hard work. I've already run further in two weeks than I have in the whole of the rest of my life put together. I've got blisters the size of Manchester!*

17

They make me eat properly – don't worry. And I haven't shot myself in the foot by accident. I'll write again soon.

Big kisses to you all,

Paul" '

Auntie Joyce looked up. Her eyes were sparkly as though she might cry, but she was smiling. Mum reached over and squeezed her arm. 'Don't worry, Joyce. He'll be OK.'

'What food is he eating?' Ruby asked, taking a brick out of Billy's mouth.

'I don't know. I don't suppose it's much different to what he gets at home. Perhaps more chips than he's used to. I'll ask him in my next letter.'

Mum reached out and stroked Billy's hair. He looked up, surprised.

Auntie Joyce sighed. 'Still. He's OK, that's the main thing. Time for a cuppa?'

Mum nodded.

Auntie Joyce dropped the letter into her huge handbag and hoisted herself out of the chair, squeezing past the counter towards the kitchen. Mum followed.

Jack smartened up the rows of twenty pences; they had been too laid-back and sloppy. General Jack Dempsey would sort out that attitude. *First Battalion Twenty Pences, reporting for duty, sir!*

Behind him, in the little kitchen, he could hear the low murmur of Mum's voice. He couldn't make out the words over the whirr of the washing machines. Auntie Joyce answered. Why were they whispering?

Because they didn't want him to hear.

Jack's hand froze above a wayward twenty pence. He held his breath.

Were they talking about Paul or about Dad?

Paul or Dad?

If it was Paul, then it was none of his business. But if it was Dad . . .

He took a step backwards, towards Mum and Auntie Joyce. On a shelf by his knees he could see the empty ice-cream tub where Mum kept pens and stray buttons and safety pins. He reached down, lifted out a pen, then dropped it on to the floor. It rolled towards the back room. Towards the kitchen.

There was a feeling in Jack's chest, like being nervous, only it wasn't that exactly. It was more insistent than that. It wasn't fair that Auntie Joyce knew more about what was going on than he did. He stepped towards the pen.

On the other side of the counter, Ruby and Billy were squabbling over a building block.

'Shh!' Jack waved them quiet. He bent down, his ears aimed at the kitchen door. He scooped up the pen, but stayed crouched.

He could hear Mum and Auntie Joyce, but their voices came in short snatches: '. . . a battlefield . . . prisoner . . . can't go on.'

Who were they talking about?

Then Auntie Joyce said, 'You can't take the world's weight on your shoulders.'

Dad then.

'Sorry . . . sorry . . .'

Jack heard Mum blow her nose.

Jack stood up quickly and dropped the pen back in the tub. He didn't want to hear any more. He stepped around the counter into the shop. His chest felt tight, as though there wasn't enough oxygen getting in. He sucked in two or three lungfuls of soapy air, then marched away from the counter and climbed up on top of the dryer, next to Lauren.

She turned the page of her magazine.

A customer walked in – a man carrying a big blue bag. He looked around and his eyes settled on Lauren, the biggest of the children.

'Service wash?' he asked hopefully.

'Mum!' Lauren yelled.

Mum appeared at the counter. Her eyes were puffy and red, but she did her best to smile. 'Can I help you?' she asked the man. He smiled gratefully and lugged his bag over.

'Mum's sad again,' Jack whispered to Lauren.

'Mmm,' Lauren agreed.

Jack looked towards the counter where Mum and the customer were busy weighing his bag of laundry.

'Couldn't we do something?' Jack said.

'Like what?' Lauren said sharply. 'I'm not doing any more chores than I do already.'

'No, not chores. I don't know. Something special. Something to make Mum and Dad happy again. To stop them rowing.'

Lauren paused. 'Something special?'

Jack nodded eagerly.

'There's a whole section in here on putting the romance back into relationships. A top ten. Look!' Lauren flipped through her magazine quickly; it was a blur of lipstick adverts and girls with daft clothes and handbags. Then she found what she wanted.

Ten Ways to Put the Spark Back

Jack leaned in and read over Lauren's shoulder. Number ten was a walk on the beach, number nine was a meal in a restaurant, number eight was – *yuck!* – numbers eight, seven and six were all gross. Number five was a balloon ride. Numbers four and three were gross too. Number two was a moonlight serenade. And number one – the number one most guaranteed way to put the spark back in any relationship – was a weekend in Paris.

'We could organise a walk on the beach, easy,' Lauren said. 'It's just at the end of the street.'

'No,' Jack said. 'The beach is there every day and they've never wanted to walk along it before. Anyway, it's the bottom one and they fight all the time. We can't go with number ten. We can't go with any of the bottom nine. It has to be number one.' He looked at the photograph next to the article. In it, a woman and a man held each other close, gazing into each other's eyes; there was a table laid with wine and candles, a man playing a violin, and above them all the Eiffel Tower rose up against a pink and gold sunset. 'If the magazine says Paris, then it has to be Paris.'

'But,' Lauren said, 'that will cost a fortune. Look.' She pointed to the bottom of the page. 'Two hundred pounds! Just for one night! Where are we going to get that sort of money? A walk on the beach is much cheaper.'

'Paris,' Jack said with determination.

CHAPTER 4

Back home, Jack called a council of war. Lauren, Ruby and Billy all crammed into his bedroom. Billy sat on the floor chewing Teddy Volvo's leg, Ruby sat on the bed and Lauren sat on the chair. Jack stood, holding Lauren's magazine open at page 32 so that everyone could see it.

'Operation Eiffel Tower,' Jack said. 'Ignore everything between number two and number ten. We are going straight to number one. Listen.' He read from the magazine, '"*You walk arm in arm down a wide boulevard; the scent of spring blossom fills the night air. You stop at a cafe; candlelit tables spill out on to the pavement. A waiter brings wine. And you? You smile at each other, remembering.*"'

Jack wrinkled his nose. 'Actually, that all sounds gross. But the important thing is that the two people here aren't arguing. They aren't throwing plates and slamming tables and keeping us all awake at night.' He prodded the people on the page.

Ruby smiled. 'It sounds pretty,' she said.

'It sounds expensive,' Lauren said.

'Two hundred pounds. We need to find two hundred pounds,' Jack said. 'That's for the train to Paris and one night in a hotel. They'll need to have dinner too. How much does dinner cost?' He looked at Lauren.

She blushed slightly, then shrugged. 'How would I know? I've never had dinner in Paris.'

'I'll ask Paul. He'll know. But we need to get at least two hundred pounds, probably more. Ideas? Anyone?'

'How many goes on the grab-a-bear machine is two hundred pounds?' Ruby asked.

Jack smiled. Then he took his calculator from his desk drawer. 'Two hundred divided by point two is one thousand. A thousand goes, Ruby.'

'A thousand?' Ruby whispered. 'That sounds like a lot.'

There was a pause while everyone thought about this. Except Billy. Billy pulled off one of his socks and tried to put it on Teddy Volvo's arm.

'It is a lot,' Lauren said.

'Yes,' Jack agreed. It was a huge, colossal, ginormous amount of money. 'But we want to make Mum and Dad happy again, don't we? We want them to stop rowing all the time about stupid things that don't matter. Don't we?'

Ruby nodded quickly.

Lauren sighed, then nodded too.

'So,' Jack said. 'How much have we got for starters? Everyone, go and get any money you have and bring it here. Now.'

Everyone stood up and charged out towards their own room.

Jack took down his piggy bank from the windowsill. It wasn't really a pig; it was a bright red London bus. Paul had brought it back for him when he'd been to London on a college trip last year. The bus felt quite heavy, but Jack knew that it was mostly just two and five pence coins.

He pulled out the white plastic plug and tipped it on to his bed.

The others came back just as he was counting out the last pile.

'Well?' Lauren asked.

'Three pounds and twenty-six pence.' Jack sighed.

Lauren was carrying a jam jar with a small roll of notes inside. 'Birthday money,' she said. 'I was saving for a hairdryer with built-in conditioner. That's twenty pounds.'

'Wow!' Jack said. 'Thanks. And what about you two?'

Billy held out a wodge of green plasticine. There was

a two-pence coin jutting out of it like a tooth. Jack grinned and took the coin.

'Ruby?' Lauren asked.

'Well,' Ruby said, 'I didn't have any money. So I had a look in Mum's purse and she had twenty pounds.' She held up a note.

'Ruby!' Jack said.

'What?'

'You can't take Mum's money to buy her a present! That's not how it works.'

'Oh.'

'Go and put it back right now. And make sure she doesn't see you. This is meant to be a nice surprise. Finding out that your daughter's a thief is not a nice surprise.'

Ruby hung her head. 'Sorry,' she whispered.

Lauren laughed. 'Don't cry about it. We'll get the money somehow.'

Ruby nodded then ran to replace the money.

Jack looked at the jar of notes and the coins on the bed. 'Twenty-three pounds and twenty-eight pence,' he said. 'Only a hundred and seventy-five pounds to go, more or less. Plus dinner.'

He sat down on the bed and the coins slid towards him. Billy crawled up next to him and started feeding his ball of plasticine to Teddy Volvo. Lauren sat down on the chair.

'Come on, people,' Lauren said. 'Ideas.'

'Sponsored walk,' Jack said. 'Sponsored silence. Or we could do odd jobs for people, like washing cars.'

Ruby danced back in. 'We could sell stuff, like on the telly.'

'We haven't got anything worth selling,' Lauren said.

Jack unscrewed the lid of Lauren's jam jar and scooped his coins inside. 'We could get a lottery ticket and win the jackpot. Or I could become a pro golfer and earn a fortune.'

Lauren grinned. 'Think you're ready to beat Tiger Woods, do you?'

'Jack can beat anyone!' Ruby said.

Jack peeled the label off the jam jar. It left behind a thin layer of white paper glued to the glass. He took a pen from his desk and wrote 'Paris Fund' on the jar.

'If I asked William,' Jack said slowly, 'if I asked him really nicely, he might hold a competition. Like a real Open. If we charge people to enter, there could be prizes – *cash* prizes. Then all I have to do is win!'

Lauren nodded slowly. 'Don't let this go to your head, but you are pretty good. Would William go for it?'

Jack nodded. 'Of course he would. We could make loads of money!'

'It could work,' Lauren said. 'It could actually work.'

CHAPTER 5

There was still just enough time before tea for Jack to go and visit William. There were hardly any players left on the course – most of them would be back at their hotels eating scampi and chips. Jack could hear the whine of a kettle on a gas stove coming from William's hut; he was taking a tea break. Jack knocked on the door.

'We're closed,' William growled from inside the hut.

'I know. It's me. I've had a genius idea,' Jack said.

'Humph!'

Jack heard William pour the water, then stir in the milk and sugar before he finally came over to the door. William's white hair had that 'just out of bed' look that Lauren spent hours doing sometimes. Jack was pretty certain that William hadn't spend hours on his version of it.

'Evening!' Jack said. 'Wouldn't it be amazing if we had an Open Championship here? We could charge everyone to enter, and give everyone scorecards, and they'd play the holes and keep score, and at the end the winner could win the entry money.'

'Evening,' William said. He took a sip of his tea. 'Say that again, much slower.'

Jack grinned. 'An Open Championship. We could have one.'

William rubbed his chin thoughtfully. Jack could hear the rasping of his fingers against stubble. 'Hmm. We could, I suppose.'

'Woo-hoo!' Jack punched the air. 'Can we do it on Saturday? In the afternoon? If we put posters up tonight, that should be enough time for people to know about it. Can first prize be two hundred pounds?'

William spluttered into his tea. 'Two hundred pounds! Do you think I'm made of money? No, it can't be two hundred pounds. Top prize fifty pounds, second prize twenty-five. And two pounds to enter. That should work. If forty people enter, I'll make five pounds.' William shook his head. 'I'd best not think about that, otherwise I'll talk myself out of it. Do you want to make a sign? I've still got some of that paint we used on the Golden Gate Bridge somewhere. And I suppose Mrs Khalid might photocopy some flyers for us.'

Jack nodded. Fifty pounds wouldn't get Mum and Dad to Paris, but it would be a great start.

CHAPTER 6

That night, Jack woke suddenly. He stared up at the ceiling. His glow-stars had faded and moonlight the colour of sour milk spilled across it.

Noises seeped up through the floorboards. Dad yelled something, Mum shouted back. Then sobs, Mum crying. Another yell. Jack closed his eyes, trying to lose himself in sleep again. But the shouts were sharp as paper-cuts, slicing through the air.

He pulled his pillow round so that it covered his face. He was hot and sweaty under its weight, but it muffled the noises. There was a small pocket of air to breathe, though he could feel it getting warmer with each breath. Soon it was mostly carbon dioxide. Jack turned his head, found more air. He rested his arm on top of the pillow, pushing it against his ears. The feathers inside crackled like burning embers. Jack hummed tunelessly.

Eventually, a long while later, he fell asleep.

CHAPTER 7

The next morning, when Jack got up, Ruby was waiting for him at the bottom of the stairs. She was rocking a pink toy pram back and forth. Occasionally she shoved so hard that the pram teetered on its side.

It was a good job the doll was reined in so tight, Jack thought.

'Jack!' she said.

'Ruby,' he said.

'I've got something to show you. Look!' Ruby held out a piece of paper.

Jack looked.

The paper was about the same size as a banknote. Ruby had coloured it pink and purple, with a lady's head on one side. With a blue felt-tip she had drawn the number '20'. Jack flipped the paper over. On the other side was a drawing of a man with folds of curly hair. Ruby had copied the £20 note from Mum's purse.

'Why have you drawn a twenty-pound note?' he asked.

'It *is* a twenty-pound note! We can put it in the Paris fund. To make Mum and Dad happy.'

'Is it meant to be a forgery?'

'What's a forgery?' Ruby asked.

'A copy.' Jack grinned. Ruby really was trying very hard. 'But this won't fool anyone,' he said.

'Yes, yes it will,' Ruby said. 'I spent ages colouring it in!' She stamped her foot and the pram shuddered at her side.

'No, Ruby, it won't. It's a lovely picture, but it just won't work.'

'How do you know? You don't know, do you?' Ruby's eyes were glistening with tears of anger.

Jack hated it when anyone cried. 'OK, listen. How about we go to the corner shop and try to buy something with it? If it works, then you can make more. If it doesn't, then we'll know.'

'Yes, OK,' Ruby said. 'Come on.'

Ruby led the way. The shop was just a few doors down. Jack had been in there about a million times – but never with a forged note. As he walked, his skin began to feel a bit prickly. Maybe this wasn't such a good idea. What if Mrs Khalid called the police? What if they went to prison? Mum and Dad would be properly furious then. They'd probably blame each other and row all night long.

By the time they reached the shop, Jack felt as though his heart was pounding in his throat.

Ruby hoisted the pram up the step and through the door. Jack followed slowly. It was cool inside. Rows of shelves stretched off towards the back, each one piled high with tins and packets and boxes. There was a freezer near the front with ice creams in it, and next to that a shelf full of magazines and newspapers. The shop always smelled of bread and floor cleaner, even though it wasn't a bakery.

Mrs Khalid was crouching in the centre aisle. She was taking tins out of a cardboard box, stamping them with the price gun and then lining them up on the shelf. She smiled as Jack and Ruby came in. Her smile made Jack feel instantly worse.

'Hello!' Ruby beamed at Mrs Khalid.

'Morning, Ruby,' Mrs Khalid said. 'Taking baby for a walk?'

Ruby nodded seriously. 'She needs the fresh air. It's not good for a baby to be cooped up all day.'

Mrs Khalid chuckled. 'Is that so?'

'Can I have a go on the price thingy?' Ruby asked, leaving the pram near the front of the shop.

'Certainly. Here, put the price on these.' Mrs Khalid held out a tin. 'It's Polish. For our new Polish section. It's cabbage, I think. I will be cooking it for my old parents, perhaps with a bit of cumin for flavour. It will make a nice change for them, don't you think? It's one pound twenty-nine. See? It's all set up – just squeeze the trigger and there's the label.'

Jack felt his face flush. He *liked* Mrs Khalid and now they were trying to pass dodgy money off on her. He swallowed and his throat felt dry.

Ruby squeezed the gun and laughed as the label shot out. She slapped it on the tin. It looked crooked from where Jack stood, but Ruby seemed happy as she put it on the shelf.

Mrs Khalid stood up and grinned. 'Now, what can I get for you two today?'

Ruby paused.

Jack frowned. They didn't actually need anything; they just wanted to see if their note would fool Mrs Khalid. He looked down at his shoes; he couldn't look Mrs Khalid in the eye.

'Er,' Ruby stammered, 'a Mars Bar ice cream and some tinfoil, please.'

Tinfoil? Jack flashed a look at Ruby and she shrugged helplessly.

Mrs Khalid picked out the things and rang them

through the till at the front of the shop. 'Do you need a bag, Ruby?'

Ruby shook her head. 'It can go in the bottom of the pram,' she said seriously.

'Of course. That will be two pounds eighty, please,' Mrs Khalid said.

This was it. This was the moment of truth. Would Mrs Khalid be fooled or would she be furious? Jack couldn't bear to look as Ruby handed over her note.

For a moment there was silence.

Then Mrs Khalid started to chuckle.

Then she laughed. Then she howled. 'Oh, Ruby Dempsey, you are a wonder!' she said. 'Did you make this? You almost fooled me. You could be a master counterfeiter!' Mrs Khalid wiped tears from her eyes. 'Oh, keep the ice cream. And the tinfoil. But you can take this money back. Hah! You've made my morning, you really have.'

'Thanks, Mrs Khalid,' Jack muttered.

Mrs Khalid sobered up a little; her expression wasn't quite so kind when she looked at Jack. 'You're old enough to know better,' she said.

'Yes, Mrs Khalid. Sorry, Mrs Khalid,' Jack said.

As they left the shop, Jack heard Mrs Khalid pick up the phone and dial. 'Oh, Maisha, you'll never believe what just happened!' she said.

Jack shook his head. This would be around the whole town in minutes. Why hadn't he thought of that?

Ruby dragged the pram behind her; she didn't speak. She handed the ice cream to Jack and held the tinfoil tightly to her chest.

'Why did you get tinfoil?' Jack asked.

'I dunno. It was the first thing I thought of.'

'Never mind,' Jack said. 'I'm sure we can think of another way to raise money.'

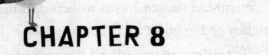

CHAPTER 8

To: jack.dempsey23@hotmail.co.uk
From: fulldinnerjacket@gmail.com
Subject: Blisters on my blisters!

Dear Jack,

What do you call a squaddie in a hedge?

Privet.

LOL! On the outside I may have the body of a weak
and knackered new recruit, but inside I'm still God's
own gift to comedy! Actually, it's a good job I have a
career as a comedian to fall back on, cos my dreams
of being Britain's Next Top Foot Model have gone
up in smoke. How can you get trench foot if you've
never even been in a trench? That's what I want to
know. I asked the Corporal and he just gave me some
athlete's foot powder. I'll let you know whether it

works, or whether I'm turning into the Creature from the Black Lagoon, with webbed toes and gammy skin. Yum.

So, in your last email you asked how much it costs to buy a fancy meal for two. Why? Is there some young lady in your life that I should know about? Someone you want to impress?

Well, if she's not all that, you could get away with spending £10 in McDonald's. But if you really want something a bit more fancy, then £40 should do it. Any more than that and she'd better be Beyoncé Knowles at the very least!

I hope that helps. Write again soon. I miss you all. I want to know what you're all up to. The thing about the army is it makes you feel like you're in a bubble – like a different world. It's easy to forget how things used to be. It seems like years since we played Snap in a den built of duvets. Do you remember that? It was only last summer. Feels like a lifetime ago.

Keep safe, God bless,

Paul

Jack closed the email. He hoped Paul was OK. Did he sound a bit sad? It was hard to tell. And £40 for a meal! As well as £200 to get to Paris in the first place. He didn't need his calculator to tell him that their jam jar didn't have anywhere near enough in it. The golf competition might help, but they also needed a Plan B. And a Plan C. And maybe even a Plan D, E and F too.

CHAPTER 9

Ruby had dumped the empty pram in the kitchen and wandered off with her doll. When Jack went to fetch a drink, he saw the tinfoil sticking out of the bottom of the pram and grinned. 'Billy!' he yelled. 'Billy, where are you?'

Billy came trotting into the kitchen, trailing Teddy Volvo by his ear and eating a biscuit.

'Ruby sort of bought some tinfoil. I've thought of something we can do with it. Do you want to play astronauts? We'll need some cardboard boxes for helmets. And some sellotape and maybe glue. Wait there!'

Billy waited there while Jack whizzed around the kitchen gathering together basic NASA supplies.

Jack cut and glued and measured and snipped the tinfoil, until the cardboard boxes were two space helmets. Then he wrapped the foil round their arms and legs so that he and Billy were wearing shiny spacesuits.

'Come in, Houston.' Jack spoke beneath his visor. 'Come in, Mission Control. One small step for a toddler, one giant leap for toddler-kind.' He lifted Billy on to the table, then swung him down in a huge gravity-defying jump. 'Mission Control, we have safely landed on this strange terrain. Commencing exploration of Planet Kitchen Floor. No sign of hostile life forms. I will now plant the flag.' Jack took three slow, careful strides then grabbed the kitchen mop and thrust it down into the bucket. 'Mission successful!' he shouted.

On the floor, Billy laughed. His helmet had fallen off. Bits of biscuit were crusted round his mouth.

'Correction, Houston. I've encountered a strange life form. Humanoid. But strangely small, stunted even, with yellow growths around its mouth. Dempsey One preparing to engage with it.'

He thought about pulling out his gun, but then he remembered his mission. Exploration. You couldn't just go shooting at every life form you met if you were an explorer.

'Greetings!' Jack said. 'I am an Earthling.'

'And I am a magic sky fairy!' Ruby's voice came from behind him.

Jack turned slowly through zero gravity. Ruby stood in the doorway. She was wearing her princess dress, the one with the bits of floaty material at the bottom. It was fancy dress, really, but Ruby wore it like ordinary clothes.

'There aren't magic sky fairies in space,' Jack said, muffled by his helmet.

'Yes there are. Space is the sky, isn't it? That's where magic sky fairies live.'

Jack sighed. 'Well, we're playing astronauts, not fairies.'

'With *my* tinfoil,' Ruby pointed out. 'Mrs Khalid gave it to me. I want to play too.'

Jack looked at the sheets of tinfoil wrapped round his trousers. Ruby was right; it kind of belonged to her. Not that she'd paid for it. 'Where's Lauren? Can't you play fairies with her?'

'Lauren's helping Mum,' Ruby said.

'Oh.'

'She's helping her get things out of the attic,' Ruby said more forcefully.

Jack frowned. The only time anyone went in the attic was when the Christmas decorations came out or the suitcases for going on holiday. Jack felt a shiver of alarm.

'What things?' he asked.

43

Ruby shook her head. 'Don't know.'

Jack lifted off his helmet and put it down on the table. 'I'll just go and see,' he told Ruby. His voice came out in a whisper, though he hadn't meant it to. 'You watch Billy for a minute. Don't let him eat the glue.'

Jack walked up the stairs. His tinfoiled legs rubbed together with a squeaky noise. The entrance to the attic was through a hole cut in the ceiling just outside the bathroom. There was a ladder propped against the opening and Lauren was standing with one foot on the bottom rung, holding it in place. One of the holiday suitcases stood on the landing; it had a thick layer of dust on it. Jack could hear dull thudding noises coming from overhead.

'What's going on?' Jack asked.

'Mum wants some stuff,' Lauren said, frowning.

'What stuff?'

Mum's feet appeared at the top of the ladder, then her legs, then Jack could see the rest of her, balancing a small box in one hand while the other gripped the frame.

'What stuff?' Jack asked again, looking at Mum this time.

Mum frowned. 'Oh, Jack,' she said.

'What's going on?' Jack asked. His chest felt tight.

'Jack, not now, OK?' Mum sounded tired. 'Lauren, I need to look through some things. Would you be a love and take them out for a while? Down to the front, just for half an hour?'

Lauren nodded. Her face looked pale and her eyes shone too bright on the dark landing.

'C'mon,' Lauren said. 'Let's get the others.' She walked towards the stairs.

Jack looked at Mum.

'Go on,' she said, not unkindly. 'Please.'

Jack followed Lauren slowly.

CHAPTER 10

'What's going on?' Jack asked Lauren as soon as they were downstairs.

'I don't know, I swear. Mum just said she needed the photo box from the attic, the one with all the birth certificates and stuff in.'

'If you don't know, why do you sound so funny?' Jack asked.

'It's just the way Mum looked, that's all. I don't like it.' She sighed heavily.

They reached the kitchen. Ruby and Billy were sitting on the floor; Ruby was gluing strips of tinfoil on to the bottom of her dress and Billy was painting the floor with gluey fingers.

'Now I'm a magic sky fairy astronaut,' Ruby said.

'Huh!' Lauren snorted. 'Everyone here is crazy except for me. Have you lot seen the state you're in? I can't take you out looking like that. You look a right show.'

Jack grinned. 'I'm US Astronaut Dempsey One, he's Dempsey Two, and Ruby is a magic sky ghost or something.'

'A magic sky fairy astronaut!'

'Whatever you are,' Lauren said, 'you can't come with me dressed like that. You look like clowns. If you go out like that, people will be asking me where they buy tickets.'

Jack laughed. Then the laughter dried up. He had thought of something. His eyes opened wide. He felt a little ripple of excitement. 'Lauren, you're brilliant. We could charge people to see us. You know, for the Paris fund.'

'What?'

'Don't you remember the lady who came last summer? The statue lady? Ruby made us go and look at her every day.'

'Oh, the ballet lady!' Ruby squealed.

Lauren nodded slowly.

Last summer, a woman had arrived on the front dressed as a ballerina. She was like a doll, standing completely still; you couldn't see her breathe, not even when you went right up close to look. She was a living statue until someone dropped a coin in her tin. Then

47

she swirled and twirled and bobbed like the ballerina in a musical box.

'We could be astronaut statues!' Jack said. 'People would pay to watch us do a space walk.' Jack put on an American accent. 'One small step for fifty pence, one giant leap for a pound.'

Lauren looked interested. Ruby clapped her hands together.

'We'll stand totally and completely still,' Jack continued, 'then when someone pays us, I could lift Billy and Ruby so it looks like they really are walking through the air. Zero-gravity statues. What do you think?' He looked at Lauren eagerly. 'We haven't put any money in the jar today. And Mum's already got the cases out. She needs a holiday. Come on, Lauren, what do you think?'

Lauren looked at Jack and Ruby who were both smiling at her. Billy's helmet had twisted round so she couldn't see his face, but he was probably keen. 'Oh fine,' she said. 'But I'm not dressing up. I can be your manager. I'll supervise. And I'll collect the money.'

They left the house, heading for the beach and the tourists.

The front was bustling with people. Families bounced along in horse-drawn carriages; couples held hands and shared ice cream. Everyone seemed to be smiling. And spending money, Jack thought hopefully. The tinfoil they wore sparkled in the sunshine, matching the glittering waves. Ruby slipped her hand through his and gave it a squeeze.

'I'm going to be a brilliant magic sky fairy,' she said. 'You can do great big jumps in space, can't you? Because of the gravy.'

'Gravity,' Jack corrected.

Ruby nodded, then leaped as high as she could. Jack tugged upwards, to give her a little lift.

They were heading for the main steps that led down on to the beach. The ice-cream van at the top of the steps was mobbed. Beyond it was William's World of Wonders. Jack could just make out the sign he'd painted for the Open Championship tomorrow. He grinned in excitement. If he did well, the Paris fund would soon be full!

'OK, here's the drill,' Lauren said, pulling Jack back from his daydream. 'You all stay really, really still. I'll collect the money in this bowl. When someone pays us, you have to act like you're walking in space. Got it?'

Jack nodded. He'd got it. Ruby nodded too. Billy chewed on Teddy Volvo's ear.

'I don't think Billy's got it,' Jack muttered.

Lauren glared at him. 'He'll just have to do his best. Right. Line up.'

Jack, Ruby and Billy formed ranks. Lauren inspected them as thoroughly as a sergeant major on a parade ground. She straightened Ruby's shoulders, she flattened the tinfoil on Jack's front, she squeezed the worst of the dribble off Teddy Volvo's ear.

'We'd best do a practice,' Lauren said. 'Ready? And . . . freeze!'

Jack froze. He was stiller than a moon rock. He was more frozen than a moon rock in a fridge-freezer. He was more silent than a sulking moon rock in a fridge-freezer.

He didn't move a muscle.

'And . . . move!' Lauren said.

Jack space-walked. He raised one foot then brought it down slowly. He walked towards Billy as though he were walking through treacle, then he scooped him up into the air with a sound like rockets blasting off. Beside him, Ruby pranced and pirouetted.

'And . . . freeze!' Lauren said.

Jack froze, with Billy suspended above his head. Oh, Billy was heavy these days! He felt his arms wobble under the weight.

'Be still!' Lauren hissed.

'I'm trying,' Jack whispered back.

Then Jack heard a fantastic noise. The chink of a coin landing in their bowl.

'Yay! Customers,' Lauren said. 'Move!'

Jack scooped Billy through the air. Billy laughed and shrieked. Ruby plié'd and twirled, kicked and jumped. She was definitely more fairy than astronaut, Jack thought.

'Freeze!'

This time Jack held Billy lower, on his shoulder, so that it was easier to keep him in the air. Billy grumbled, eager to be flown around again.

'Shh,' Jack hissed. 'Wait for the money!'

They didn't have long to wait. Lots of people stopped and dropped a coin into the bowl. Soon he could hear each one clinking down on to what sounded like a good pile.

'Hey!' A voice sounded cross. 'Hey, you!'

Jack wondered whether to unfreeze and look. He decided to wait for instructions from Lauren.

'Hey! This is my spot!'

'What's your spot?' Lauren said.

'Here. By the ice-cream van.'

'Who says?'

'The council. All the performers get a spot, and this one is mine. If you want one, you have to go and ask them.'

Jack had had enough of standing still and not looking, so he moved. Lauren was standing next to a boy.

He was older than they were, but not quite a grown-up yet. He held a guitar looped on a strap round his neck. He had blond hair and tanned skin, as though he'd spent the whole summer outside. On this spot.

'You weren't here when we started. Finders keepers,' Lauren said.

'No, permits keepers. I've got a permit. I get to keep the spot. You lot have to shift.'

'We're not going!' Lauren said.

The boy laughed. 'Fine. We'll see what the police have to say.'

'Lauren,' Jack warned.

'We're statues,' Ruby told the boy.

He looked at her. He nodded. 'I see. But you can't be statues here. Sorry.'

'But we need the money for Paris,' Ruby said.

'I need the money to buy dinner tonight,' the boy said.

Jack looked down at the tiny dunes of sand that gathered in the corner of each step. He sighed. 'Maybe we've made enough money anyway.' His arms were getting tired from lifting Billy.

Lauren shook the bowl, then snorted. 'Hardly. But I s'pose it will have to do. For now.'

The boy grinned at her. Did he wink? Lauren's cheeks went a bit pink. Then she grabbed the handle of Billy's pram and pulled it violently. She turned round and started pushing it back in the direction of the house.

'Wait for us!' Jack called.

As they raced after Lauren, Jack heard the sound of strumming behind him as the boy began his first song.

CHAPTER 11

They were back at the house in minutes. Lauren had run ahead. Jack held Billy close as he and Ruby chased behind her. They turned the corner into their street.

Then Jack stopped.

He stood still, looking at the house.

'What is it?' Ruby whispered.

Jack shook his head. He walked forward slowly. It felt as though the air was too dense and he had to force his legs through it. Lauren stood with the empty pram at the garden gate.

'Lauren?' Ruby asked. 'What's going on?'

There was a suitcase next to the step. And a black bin bag. The front door was open. There was a noise from inside. The sound of the night-time shouting, come like an intruder into the day. A noise like pain.

'They're arguing,' Lauren said.

Jack waited with the others near the gate. The children were silent. Listening, but trying not to hear, trying not to understand Mum and Dad. The shouting voices twisted, overlapping, neither able to hear the other through the noise of it all. Jack stood on the pavement, his hand on Ruby's shoulder holding her back. He didn't want to go inside. Not now, not ever.

There was a sudden silence.

Dad came out.

He was carrying two plastic bags. Jack could see a black sock hanging over the edge of one of the bags. He focused on it; he could see the ribs of stitching, the bobbles in the wool where it had been washed too often in a hot wash.

Dad picked up the suitcase. It wobbled and nearly fell. He piled the plastic bags on top and tried to hold everything in one hand. He grabbed the bin bag with the other hand.

Jack looked down. He didn't want to see Dad's face.

'What's happening?' Ruby asked.

The sock dropped from the bag to the ground, but Dad didn't notice. Lauren reached down, picked it up and tucked it back into the bag. Dad looked as though he wanted to say something. He paused and then he just whispered, 'Thanks.'

'Dad, where are you going?' Ruby said.

'I don't know,' Dad said. 'I'll call you when I get there, OK?'

Billy wriggled in Jack's arms, trying to reach out as Dad passed.

Dad didn't speak; he carried on out of the gate and down the road. Jack watched him – the way the bags bumped against his knees, the way he tried to steer the suitcase with his foot, the way the muscles flexed beneath his T-shirt.

Jack felt Ruby's hand in his, icy cold despite the sunshine. He squeezed it gently and pulled Billy closer with his other arm.

Jack felt hollow, as though his insides had just dissolved. He could feel Ruby's hand and he could see Lauren's eyes, but that was all. Nothing else made any sense.

Then Mum came to the door, 'All of you. Inside. Now.'

Ruby pulled him inside, the pram left abandoned on the path. Lauren stood for a little longer, but Mum barked her name and so she came in too.

The house seemed horribly quiet.

Mum said nothing; she went into the front room and closed the door behind her.

'What's going on?' Ruby whispered.

Jack looked down at her. 'Dad's left,' he said. 'They've split up.' The sound seemed to come from far away, as though it was someone lost speaking.

'For good?'

'I don't know. Maybe.'

'But what about Paris?'

Jack went up to his room. He peeled off what was left of the tinfoil. He had to sit, just sit and be by himself. He felt sick. He didn't turn on his computer, he didn't do anything. He just held himself still and small, like water cupped in his hands, trying not to let it drain away. Eventually the room got darker. He heard sounds from downstairs, maybe crying, maybe just talking. He pulled in one breath and let it out again. Night was coming. Night was coming and Dad wasn't here.

'Jack?' Auntie Joyce's voice whispered outside his door. When had she arrived?

'Jack? Can I come in?'

'Yes.' His voice still sounded strange, as though there was a bubble of water trapped in his ears. Last term at school, his teacher had told the class that his body was made of 70 per cent water. He felt as though it were true, as though his insides were liquid, sloshing against his skin. *Could you drown inside yourself?*

The door opened. 'It's time to come and eat. You have to eat something. Come downstairs, please.'

Jack got up. He felt himself move, though he didn't know how it was happening.

57

In the kitchen, Lauren and Ruby sat in front of plates of fish fingers and mash. Billy, in his high chair, picked at a bowl of the same stuff.

'Where's Mum?' Jack asked, slipping into his seat.

'In her room, poor thing.' Auntie Joyce clicked her tongue. 'I'll take hers up. But you, you eat at the table.' She spoke firmly, taking charge.

Jack looked at the orange crumbs around the fish. He cut it open and stared at the white flesh, shiny and wet-looking.

'Eat it, don't play with it,' Auntie Joyce said. She ran a bowl of hot water at the sink.

He lifted a forkful up to his mouth as though he were a machine.

It was Ruby who asked the question they all wanted to ask. 'Auntie Joyce, when is Dad coming back?'

Auntie Joyce splashed some cutlery into the washing-up bowl. 'I can't say, sweetheart. That's up to your mum and dad, not me.'

'But where has he gone?'

'I heard he was going to a B and B,' Auntie Joyce said. 'I expect he'll be in touch once he's settled. Right now you all have to be good kids, help your mum out as much as you can. She's going to need you to be brave.'

Jack dropped his fork back on to his plate. He couldn't stand this. He stood and left the kitchen.

Down the hall, up the stairs, into his room. He closed the door and leaned against it heavily. He sank down, with his back jammed up against the door. He rested his forehead on his knees and just concentrated on breathing. One breath in, one breath out, again and again. His lungs felt tight, as though they would never fill with air again.

There was a tap on his door. It would be Auntie Joyce or, worse, Ruby. 'Go away,' he said.

'Jack? It's me.' Lauren.

His big sister.

Jack suddenly wanted to see her more than anyone, more than Dad, even. He sprang up and opened the door.

In the darkness of the hall, Lauren looked thin and shadowy. She was carrying a glass of milk, with strawberry mix in it. 'Here,' she said, passing it to him.

Jack stepped back to let her into the room.

She dropped down on to his bed, half-sitting, half-lying. 'It had to happen sometime,' she said finally.

'Did it?'

'They've been rowing for months, you know that.' Lauren sounded angry.

Jack nodded. Of course he had heard them. But that didn't mean that he'd expected this, not really. 'What are we going to do?'

'You heard Auntie Joyce. We have to help Mum and we have to not be any trouble. And we have to hope Dad rings.' Lauren kicked Jack's bed frame with her trainer. It made a dull ringing noise like a broken bell.

'Paris,' Jack said. 'We need to carry on with the Paris fund. If they can spend a weekend together, without the stress, then they might be able to sort it out. They never have time together. We're always around, me or you or Ruby or Billy. We need to send them away from us.'

'We're not the problem!'

'Aren't we? Ruby thinks there are too many of us. If it wasn't for all of us, there'd be more money, less stress. Perhaps she's right. If they didn't have four kids to worry about, then perhaps they'd like each other more.'

'Ruby was just saying that because she still wishes Billy wasn't here. You know that. She's always been jealous.'

'She *was* the baby,' Jack said.

'She *is* a baby!' Lauren said.

'Don't fight. I don't want to fight,' Jack said. He sat down on the bed next to Lauren. She shuffled up to make room. Jack half-wished that she'd put her arm round him, tell him that it was going to be all right.

'OK,' she said. 'We won't fight.'

'How much is in the jar after doing statues?'

Lauren shrugged. 'I don't know. About forty pounds, I think.'

'And I've got the golf competition tomorrow. If I win, we'll have ninety pounds in the jar. Nearly half-way there! We have to carry on.'

'OK. Yes. We'll raise the money. But, I don't know if it will help, not really.'

'But we have to try!' Jack insisted.

'Fine. We'll try,' Lauren said.

CHAPTER 12

That night Jack lay in bed, staring up at the glow-stars stuck to his ceiling. He was trying not to think about Dad. He was sure that everyone else was awake too; the house just didn't feel restful – it was as though even the walls were holding their breath to see what would happen next.

His door opened at about midnight. Ruby. She trailed her duvet behind her and curled up on the bottom of his bed, like a cat. He didn't mind. It was nice to feel her there, warm and heavy on his toes.

'Where do you think Dad is?' Ruby whispered into the darkness.

'I don't know.'

'He's not sleeping outside though?'

Jack shook his head. Then he remembered that Ruby couldn't see him in the dark. 'Of course he isn't.

He'll have gone to stay on someone's sofa. Or a hotel or something. He won't be outside. He'll call us tomorrow – I'm sure he will.'

And Jack tried his best to be sure. Dad couldn't just disappear, could he? The plastic stars were slowly fading now, losing their light. Jack turned his face into the pillow and tried to get to sleep.

Lauren was already dressed and sitting at the kitchen table when Jack got up. He walked into the room, rubbing his eyes. He took a bowl from the draining board and helped himself to cereal.

'Morning,' Jack said.

Lauren said nothing. Jack added milk to his bowl. He twirled his spoon round so that the milk turned chocolatey brown.

'I tried ringing Dad last night,' Lauren said.

Jack chewed his cereal thoughtfully.

'But he didn't answer. I got voicemail.'

'Did you leave a message?' Jack asked.

'I didn't know what to say.' She looked at her phone. It lay silent next to her plate.

'He'll see the missed call though. He'll ring, won't he?' Jack asked.

They ate without speaking. When Lauren finished she pushed back her chair; it scraped along the lino.

'Where's Mum? Is she up?' Jack asked.

Lauren shook her head. 'She took a sleeping pill at about three o'clock in the morning. I bumped into her on the landing last night.'

'Did she say anything?' Jack asked.

'Like what?'

'Like where Dad is. Like whether he's coming back.'

'Jack, it was three o'clock in the morning.' Lauren sighed.

'So?'

'So she didn't say much of anything.'

Jack chewed his cereal. Lauren stared at the table.

'It's the Golf Open Championship today,' Jack said. 'I could win fifty pounds to put in the Paris fund.'

'Oh yes, I suppose you might. What time does it start?' Lauren asked.

'Two o'clock.'

'What if Dad rings? What if he wants to see us?' Lauren said quietly.

'He'll ring this morning, won't he? He said he'd ring as soon as he could. He has to!'

Lauren stood up. She slipped her phone into her pocket. 'I'm going to get Billy so he doesn't wake Mum. Wash your bowl, OK?'

Jack nodded.

64

He rinsed his bowl under the tap. He didn't know what to do next. He felt a horrible tightness in his chest, like breathing in water. What did people do when their dads were missing? He gripped the hard edge of the sink and waited for the feeling to pass.

It did. Slowly.

He'd win the competition later and Dad would be OK.

He could hear Lauren coming back downstairs with Billy in her arms. They came into the kitchen. Billy's face was still red from sleep, his hair sticking out, his eyes crusty. Jack suddenly wanted to whisk him away and keep him safe somewhere.

Lauren dropped him into his high chair.

'I'll go and see what Ruby's doing,' Jack said.

He went upstairs. Ruby was in her own bed; she must have crept back there before dawn. The curtains were still closed and the light was pinky-red. He drew them back, letting real sunshine in.

Ruby moaned from under her duvet.

'Morning, Ruby,' Jack said.

'Daddy?' Her voice was thick with sleep.

'No,' Jack said. 'It's just me. Dad hasn't called yet, but it's early. He will. Come on, sleepyhead.'

Ruby followed Jack down into the living room. Lauren and Billy drifted in soon after. They sat in front

65

of the telly watching cartoons. Only Billy laughed at them.

One programme turned into another. Then another.

Jack looked at the sunlit road just outside the window. It was a good morning for golf, but he didn't move. He didn't even get dressed. It was the same feeling as when he sat outside the dentist's office, hearing the drill going and knowing it was his turn next.

Then, just before ten o'clock, the phone rang.

'Daddy! Daddy! Daddy!' Ruby leaped up from the sofa and pelted into the hall towards the phone. 'Daddy!' she said into the receiver.

Jack ran after her. Lauren swept Billy up too and followed behind. Ruby was listening carefully and nodding.

'Is it him?' Lauren said. 'Let me speak to him.'

Ruby clung tighter to the phone and pressed it against her ear. 'Yes, yes. No. Lauren and Jack. And Billy. When are you coming home? Hey!'

Lauren had snatched the phone. Ruby's scream of outrage was loud enough to wake the dead. She tried to kick Lauren, but Jack pulled her back just in time. 'Let Lauren have a turn too,' he whispered.

'Dad? Where are you?' Lauren said. She listened for a minute, then made agreeing noises.

Jack tried to catch her eye – it was his turn now.

But Lauren just twirled the cord round her finger and listened. Finally, she hung up.

'Lauren!' Jack couldn't help himself.

'What?'

'I didn't speak to him!'

'Well, you will later. He told me where he's staying. He says we can visit. We can go as soon as Mum wakes up.'

There was a creak on the stairs. 'Did I hear my name?'

Jack looked up. Mum was coming down, her dressing gown wrapped tight around her. Her hair was flat where she'd been lying on it.

'Mummy!' Ruby ran up the stairs as though it had been weeks since she'd last seen her.

'Morning, sweet pea,' Mum said. 'I need a cup of tea. Have you all had breakfast?'

They followed Mum into the kitchen. Jack watched her fill up the kettle, then flick it on. She dropped a tea bag into a mug, then leaned against the counter waiting for the water to boil. Just as though it were a normal day. Jack felt his chest tighten again. 'That was Dad on the phone,' he said.

Mum paused for a moment. Then she said, 'How was he?'

'I don't know. I didn't talk to him.'

'He sounded sad,' Ruby said quickly.

'Oh.' Mum poured the hot water on the tea bag and stirred it. She fished the bag out and put it on a saucer next to the kettle that already had loads of dried-up tea bags on it, like mouldy pebbles. Mum rubbed her face with both hands, then pulled her fingers through her hair. She took the milk out of the fridge and stirred it into the tea.

There was silence. Jack looked at the ground. There was a blob of something sticky on the floor near his toe – old marmalade or something. He pressed his slipper on to it then lifted it with a ripping noise.

'He's staying at a bed and breakfast near town. He says we can visit him today,' Lauren said.

'What?' Mum asked. 'Where?'

'Near the real golf course. The Larches, it's called. He told me when he rang. We're going there later. It's all arranged.'

'But you can't,' Mum said. 'It's too soon. Dad and I have to talk about this first. He can't just go and take you away somewhere.'

'He's not taking us away,' Lauren said.

The crease between Mum's eyes deepened. 'I don't know that, do I? What's it like, this place he's staying? Is it safe? Is it clean? I don't know anything about it. I can't just let you go there by yourselves. And, I . . . I'm not ready to see him. Not yet.'

Lauren seemed to swell with anger. 'Well, you should have thought of that before you kicked him out, shouldn't you?'

'Lauren! That's not how it was,' Mum said, her face draining of colour.

'Well, what was it like then? He chose to leave, did he? He decided he'd had enough of us all? That we were getting on his nerves?' Lauren pushed a chair and it clattered heavily against the table. 'I'm going to visit Dad, and you can't stop me!'

'Lauren. Wait!' Mum said. But Lauren had already left the kitchen. Jack heard her stamping her way up the stairs.

'I'll go after her, Mum. Don't worry,' Jack said.

Jack climbed the stairs two at a time. He tapped gently on her door. 'Lauren, it's me. Can I come in?'

'No! Go away!'

'Please?'

There was a pause, then the door opened. 'What do you want?' Lauren's teary face peered out at him.

'Nothing.'

Lauren relaxed slightly. 'Then what are you bothering me for?'

'No reason.'

Lauren smiled properly. Then a frown creased her forehead. 'I'm going anyway, you know. She can't stop me. Dad's all by himself in some grotty place –'

'We don't know it's grotty,' Jack interrupted.

'He's all alone in some grotty, smelly, ugly place and she won't even let us visit. Well, it's not fair. I'm going and I don't care what she says.' Lauren disappeared into her room. Jack followed cautiously. She pulled her trainers out from under her bed and tugged them on to her feet.

'You're going now?' Jack asked.

'Yes. Coming?'

'Yes. No. Should we tell Mum?'

'No,' Lauren shook her head. 'She'd only try and stop us. We'll tell her when we get back.'

'What about the competition?'

'Don't worry, we'll be back in plenty of time for that.'

Jack paused, then nodded. He rushed into his room and pulled on some clothes. Then he followed Lauren down to the front door, where his trainers were balanced on top of a jumbled pile of shoes. 'We're just nipping out, Mum,' he yelled towards the kitchen.

Ruby appeared in the kitchen doorway. 'Where are you going?' she asked, her eyes wide with alarm.

Poor thing, Jack thought. She must be worried that everyone's leaving her. 'Just to the shops,' he said. 'Lauren needs a few things. And I thought she could do with getting out for a bit.'

'Can I come?' Ruby asked.

'No. You can't walk quick enough. But we won't be long. Promise. We'll bring you back something.'

'No!' Ruby wailed. Mum appeared beside her.

'We won't be long, Mum,' Jack said. 'Lauren just needs some fresh air.'

Mum nodded silently, then pulled Ruby into a hug. Ruby let herself be cuddled. 'I'm sorry,' Jack heard Mum whisper, but he wasn't sure who she was talking to. Mum carried Ruby back into the kitchen.

Lauren threw a dirty look at the space where they'd been. Then she opened the front door and they were outside, in bright sunlight.

'Do you know where the B and B is?' Jack asked.

'Yes. Dad told me. We walk to the front and along the parade. It's just past the end. Should take us about fifteen minutes.'

Jack stopped walking. 'Should we take anything? Does Dad need clean clothes or a toothbrush or anything?'

'He didn't say. I think he just wants us. Come on.'

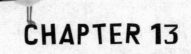

CHAPTER 13

The road outside was busy with children playing and old people walking to the shops. But there
was a heavy feeling on Jack's heart that meant he
didn't want to talk to any of the people who waved
at them.

Was Dad OK? Jack knew it had only been a day, but
Dad had been on his own, surrounded by strangers,
away from his family for all that time. He suddenly
had an awful thought: what if Dad had cried himself
to sleep last night?

Jack gasped. He stopped still.

'Come on,' Lauren said crossly, pulling his arm.

Jack stumbled but carried on walking. He wished
there was someone he could talk to about this pain. If
only Paul were still here. Emails just weren't the same.
Why did everyone feel so far away?

The bed and breakfast, when they got there, was part of a row of three. They all had signs hanging in the front gardens with a small white plaque saying 'Vacancies'. There was 'Sunnybank', 'Abbeywood' and then 'The Larches'.

'See, it looks grotty,' Lauren said.

Jack looked at the hanging baskets of flowers beside the door. They had dried and shrivelled to brown husks. The paint around the window frames had been white but was now chipped and yellow. It was hideous.

'Should we go in?' Jack asked.

'Well, we didn't come all this way for the view,' Lauren said. She marched up to the front door and pushed. It wasn't locked. There was a narrow hallway, with two doors on the left and two on the right. One door had *Reception* painted on it in black letters. The hall smelled fusty, like damp sheets.

Lauren pushed the Reception door. It was locked.

'Look,' Jack said pointing to the side of the frame. 'Ring the doorbell.'

Lauren rang the bell and they heard a faint buzzing somewhere far behind the door. Jack felt himself grow more and more miserable. Dad didn't belong here. It wasn't fair.

The door opened. A woman with bright red hair and blue eyeshadow grinned at them. 'Help you?' she asked. Her voice was gravelly as though she smoked too much.

'We're looking for our dad,' Lauren said.

'Blimey, that's a new one. Got a name, have you?'

'Gavin. Gav Dempsey. He came here yesterday.'

'Oh. Yes. Room four. Up the stairs, third on the left, past the loo.'

'Thanks.'

Jack followed Lauren up the stairs. The carpet was red with big swirly patterns, but it had worn down to the brown threads on the edge of each stair. He breathed carefully, in and out. It felt as though there was a bird fluttering in his chest.

The third door had a black and gold number stuck right in the middle of it – '4'.

Lauren knocked.

When Dad opened the door, Jack felt such a rush of relief that it was hard to remember what he had been scared of. Dad's grin was as wide as ever. He smelled of the same spicy warm smell that he always had. He was Dad. Jack tumbled into him. Strong arms wrapped round him in a bear hug.

'Oh, you two are a sight for sore eyes,' Dad said finally as he let them go.

'Hi, Dad,' Lauren mumbled.

'Come in, come in.' Dad stepped aside and they

walked into his new room. Jack looked around. There was a double bed with a flowery pink cover, all ruffled from Dad sleeping there, a chest of drawers with a TV on it, a kettle, a few ugly glass ornaments, a wardrobe and two pictures on the walls, one of a boat during a storm, the other of a couple dancing on a beach.

Dad sat down on the bed. Lauren looked for somewhere to sit, but there wasn't a chair. She went and stood by the window, looking out over a small car park at the back. Jack sat down on the bed next to Dad. Dad reached out and put his arm round Jack's shoulders and pulled him into a hug. After a while, he whispered, 'Good lad,' into Jack's hair. Then he looked up. 'Cup of tea?' he asked. 'Or coffee? I've got little individual sachets of milk. But you'll have to share a cup.'

Jack shook his head. So did Lauren.

'Well,' Dad said.

Lauren and Jack glanced at each other, then looked away quickly.

'Well,' Dad said again. 'How is everyone? How's your mum?'

'OK.'

'And Ruby and Billy? They couldn't come with you?'

'No, they weren't allow—' Lauren paused. 'They couldn't come. They were busy. They'll come next time.'

Jack frowned. There were too many lies flying about the place, like midges, getting in his eyes and mouth. He wanted to spit.

'They're busy?' Dad asked. He didn't sound like he believed Lauren.

She nodded.

Dad didn't say anything.

'Is it OK here?' Jack asked finally.

'Oh, it's OK. The breakfast was good this morning. It will do until I find something better.'

'Are you coming back?' Jack blurted. Lauren scowled at him.

'I . . . I don't know, son. Not for a bit at least. Me and your mum – well, it just isn't working at the minute. Look, let me get you some tea.'

Dad stood up and started messing around with the kettle. He had his back to them and Jack thought he looked stiff and awkward, as though he didn't know what to do with himself.

'It's complicated,' Dad suddenly said softly. 'Me and Caro, we just – I don't know. It isn't like it used to be, that's all. When we were young, when the dinosaurs roamed the earth, it was fun. We laughed a lot.'

Jack found that hard to imagine.

Dad squeezed a tea bag against the side of the mug and dropped it into the bin. He opened a tiny plastic carton and poured the milk in. 'The day I asked her to marry me – it's right up there in the top five days of my life. I got her this tiny diamond ring – it was all I could afford then. But she took it and wore it for a year before we'd saved up enough to get married.'

'I remember,' Lauren said.

'Of course, sweetheart. You were my little princess then. You still are. You were so sweet in your bridesmaid's dress. And Paul was a pageboy. Seems like a lifetime ago. That day was the number one day of my life. Your mum looked beautiful. And I swapped the diamond ring for a gold one and we danced the first dance in front of everyone. Then – do you remember, Lauren? – I got up with the band and sang to her. It was a surprise. She did most of the planning for the wedding but she didn't know about that. I got up and sang 'Love Me Tender'. It was an old song even then, but it was just right.' Dad started singing the first few lines of the song, but his voice cracked and shook too much to hear the tune properly.

Jack looked at the dark brown tea Dad gave him. He didn't want to drink it, but he didn't want to put it down either. He just held the mug and stared. A film of grease floated on the top.

'Look, Dad,' Lauren said, 'can we go for a walk or something? No offence, but it's depressing in here.'

'Of course,' Dad said quietly. 'We can take a walk on the front.'

'No,' Jack said suddenly. He wasn't sure why, but he felt like he didn't want to see the families on the beach today. He handed the mug of tea to Lauren. 'Can't we just stay here for a bit?' he asked.

Lauren took the tea, then shrugged. 'Fine.'

Jack wriggled off his trainers then leaned back on the bed. It smelled of Dad. He bundled the corner of the blanket into a ball and held it close to his chest. He was as bad as Billy with Teddy Volvo, but he didn't care. He tucked his legs up to his tummy so that his whole body was wrapped round the bedclothes.

'Tired, son?' Dad asked. 'We could stay here and watch a bit of telly. I get three and a half channels on this bad boy.' Dad patted the old square TV at the end of the bed.

Jack wondered what they had talked about before, him and Dad, before Dad moved out. It was only a day ago, but Jack couldn't focus. But he knew, he *knew* that it hadn't felt like this. It hadn't been awkward and uncomfortable. He had just thrown himself down on the sofa next to Dad and stolen a crisp or a biscuit and watched TV. Or he'd kicked a ball against the back wall while Dad mowed the grass. He had been like the moon and Dad was the earth – they didn't need to *say* anything, they were just *there* together. Now the earth was out of orbit and Jack was spinning round nothing. He shouldn't have to try to think of things to say to his own dad!

'Yes,' Jack said. 'We could watch telly.'

Lauren came and sat up by the pillows, her trainers kicked off on to the floor. Dad sat at the end of the bed, fiddling with the channels. An old film came on. Posh-voiced men in uniforms talked about war, command chains and attack fronts. Jack's eyes closed.

When he opened his eyes, the light in the room had changed. The sunlight was warm orange instead of bright white. Jack stretched, he must have fallen asleep.

He suddenly remembered the competition.

He sat up. 'What time is it?'

Dad was sitting next to him, cradling a can of pop. He turned and smiled. 'You back with us? Great visitor you turned out to be. You missed almost all of *Bridge on the River Kwai*.'

'Why? What time is it?'

Dad passed the can of pop to Jack, then looked at his watch. 'It's a quarter to two.'

Fifteen minutes until the competition started. He just had time to get there, if he was quick. Jack slugged back some pop, it was a bit warm, but still fizzy. Better than another cup of greasy tea.

'Where's Lauren?' Jack asked. She wasn't in the room.

'She's nipped to the loo. The film's not her kind of thing, maybe.'

On screen, the music was all tense. Someone was going to get shot any minute. 'Dad,' Jack said, 'we have to go.'

'But – but the film hasn't finished.'

Jack couldn't look Dad in the eye, he sounded too sad. 'I know, but I have to go. There's something I have to do.'

Dad took back his drink. 'Will you come again tomorrow? Maybe bring Billy and Ruby?'

'I don't know. Depends what Mum says.'

Dad's shoulders stiffened. 'How do you mean?'

'I don't know if she'll let them come. She . . . she didn't want me and Lauren to come today.'

The bedroom door opened and Lauren walked in.

'Is this right?' Dad asked her. 'Your mum doesn't want you visiting me?'

Lauren flashed Jack a dirty look. Then she half-shrugged. 'Yeah.'

Something in Dad's face seemed to crumple. Jack looked down at his hands. He flexed his fingers a few times; his knuckles crunched.

'We should go now,' Jack said to Lauren quietly. 'I've got that thing.'

Lauren nodded. 'We'll try and come again,' she said to Dad. 'We'll try.'

There was a long pause, then Dad stood up. 'OK, give me a hug before you go.'

As they said goodbye, Jack held Dad tight. But in the end he had to let go.

CHAPTER 14

'How long have we got before the competition starts?' Jack asked once they were outside. Lauren pulled out her phone and checked the time.

'Ten minutes.'

Jack grinned at Lauren. 'Race you!'

He started running, slowly at first to make sure that Lauren was running alongside him. Then faster, slamming his feet down as hard as he could. There seemed to be no sounds in the world except for his heartbeat and his footsteps, pounding in time. The world whipped past, colour and shapes just blurring like one of Billy's paintings. He felt as if the wind was chasing all his thoughts clean out of his head.

He beat Lauren to the entrance by three paces.

'You had a head start,' she panted, clutching a stitch in her side.

'Did not. I just beat you, that's all. And I'll beat you in the Open too!'

'Me?' Lauren's eyebrows shot up. 'I'm not playing!'

'Yes, you are. If I come first and you come second, then we win seventy-five pounds. With the money from statues, that means we'd be more than halfway to our total.'

'But I haven't played for ages.'

'Time you did then. Come on. I borrowed some money from the Paris fund so we can both enter.'

'You did what?'

'Lauren, you have to speculate to accumulate.' Jack grinned. 'Let's go and check out the competition!'

Lauren followed him down to William's hut. There were loads of people milling around – families and people in ones and twos. They all held scorecards and clubs.

William scowled when he saw Jack. 'See how much extra work you've made. Look at all these people. Forty-one entrants so far.'

'Well, it's forty-three now with me and Lauren,' Jack said, dropping four coins on to the counter. 'And can I have my lucky putter?'

William sighed and reached for Jack's favourite club. 'Mrs Khalid has come down to help. Her nephew's minding the shop. I'd have been in a right old mess without her. Though she says I need to hold heats and qualifying rounds next year. Next year!' William shook his head in disgust.

Mrs Khalid had taken charge. She was handing out scorecards and smiling at everyone. At two o'clock she stood up on a crate so that everyone could see her. 'Welcome,' she said. 'Here's how this will work. You will play in groups of four or five. Everyone will begin by playing nine holes. You will record your own scores on a card, but the card must be signed by all the players in your group – that means no cheating.' The crowd laughed a bit sheepishly. 'After nine holes, we will see who has the best score. All players within ten points of the leader will go on to play the remaining nine holes. At the end of the competition, the winner will receive fifty pounds as a prize. Second place will receive twenty-five pounds. May the best player win!'

Mrs Khalid called out everyone's names, dividing them into their groups. Lauren stood on the edge of their group, swinging her club at a blade of grass. Jack smiled at the two other people they'd be playing with – a girl and a boy. Jack guessed that they were somewhere in age between him and Lauren. The girl had mousy brown hair pulled back in a ponytail. The boy had black hair and dark eyes. He smiled at Jack.

'I'm Ali,' the boy said. 'And this is my stepsister Caitlin.'

'Hi. I'm Jack. That's Lauren. I haven't seen you around before,' Jack said.

'We're just on holiday,' Ali replied. 'Last year we went to France, but it's nice here too.'

Jack smiled at Ali. Both Lauren and Caitlin frowned.

They took their position at the Great Pyramid – a par four.

'That means you have four goes to get the ball in the hole, Caitlin,' Lauren said.

'Thanks, but we've been playing here all week. I know what par four means,' Caitlin said. 'I'll go first.'

Caitlin placed her ball on the tee and gave a few practice swings before she chipped it up. It was clear to Jack that she knew what she was doing. The ball rolled gently between the paws of the Sphinx before curving round to face the stepped walls of the Pyramid.

Jack whistled between his teeth. She was a player.

Lauren went next. Her ball bounced hard against the Sphinx's eye before landing back practically at her feet.

'Oops!' she said.

Ali took his first shot. His ball didn't make it through the gap either.

Then it was Jack's turn. He took deep, slow breaths and let the weight of the club settle in the middle of his palm. He swung gently, striking the ball in just the right spot. The ball leaped off the tee and swept easily through the Sphinx's paws.

He and Caitlin were level.

They had to wait until Ali and Lauren managed to get their balls on to the green before they could take their turn again. After three shots Lauren was through the obstacle; four shots later, Ali joined them.

Jack was aiming right for the hole now, up the ramp on one side of the pyramid and down into the King's Chamber. He wiggled his hips and bent his knees, just to keep loose. Then he swung. The ball rolled straight and true up the ramp, before dropping smoothly into the hole. Jack smiled – two under par for the first hole.

Then Caitlin took her shot. It was an exact replica of Jack's and landed just as smoothly. They were neck and neck.

He won the next hole with one under; Caitlin was on par.

He was out in front until the Leaning Tower of Pisa. His ball bounced off the wonky side and Caitlin took the lead.

All around them, other players whooped or sighed as their balls landed in the holes or in the water. Lauren had knocked up a total that was more like a netball score than a golf one and Ali was no better.

But Jack and Caitlin were battling properly now. They were within one score of each other after every hole. They finished the first nine holes with their score tied. Caitlin scribbled her name on Ali's scorecard as though she wished the pen would tear it in half.

When everyone had finished the first round, Mrs Khalid called all the players together. 'I'll take a few minutes to look at the scorecards,' she shouted. 'Then we'll see which players will make the cut and move on to the next round.'

Jack sat chewing his nails, waiting for the decision. Lauren ran over to the ice-cream van to fetch a cone for them to share. Caitlin and Ali sat close by. Jack had the feeling that Ali would have liked to chat, if only Caitlin wasn't glaring at him. She really wanted to win, Jack realised. But then, so did he.

'Right,' Mrs Khalid said. 'We have two current leaders. Jack Dempsey and Caitlin O'Connor are tied in first place. There are eight other players within ten points of them, so the following players will make the cut and go through to the next round: Stefan Kalinowski, Erin Jones . . .'

Jack felt a tingle of delight that spread up to the tips of his ears – he was through! And in joint first place. He let Lauren finish the ice cream while he listened carefully to Mrs Khalid read the rest of the names.

'. . . Max Ottar, David Andrews, Ashleigh Barrow, Jonnie Downend, Freya South, Naveen Qureshi.'

Lauren wasn't on the list. Jack sighed. He wasn't really surprised, but it did mean that he had to win, or at least come second, if they were to take home any money at all.

Lauren popped the wafer tip of the cone into her mouth and crunched it. 'Don't worry,' she said. 'You're good enough for both of us.'

Jack bit the inside of his lip. Was he?

'OK, everyone,' William shouted. 'Will the players please make their way to the Golden Gate Bridge, hole ten. You'll play the final holes in pairs, with those furthest behind the leaders going first. Freya South and Naveen Qureshi, that means you.'

The crowd surged towards the final holes, everyone jostling for a good view. Jack walked up slowly. He would be paired with Caitlin and they would go last.

Freya and Naveen were both nervous in front of the crowd. They took far too many shots to finally putt the ball. Freya, a girl with long blonde plaits, held her head down as she walked to the next hole.

Most of the other players were the same, there was something about being watched that made the clubs seem too heavy, the shafts too slippery, the balls smaller than an ant's eyeball.

Then it was Jack and Caitlin's turn.

Jack looked up at William, who winked quickly. Then he struck the ball. It ran straight along the elegant span of the bridge and dropped right in the middle of the green on the other side. Perfect.

Caitlin's shot was even better. It rolled on to the green, bounced hard off the back wall and cannoned into the hole. A hole-in-one! A totally fluky hole-in-one, but still a hole-in-one.

Jack's heart sank. Caitlin had leaped ahead of him on the scoreboard. He putted his ball smoothly, but didn't smile at the polite applause. He saw Lauren in the crowd giving him a thumbs-up. He nodded to her. He could do this.

In front of them the other players had stretched out along the course, with the crowd cheering them on – the Grand Canyon, the Taj Mahal, Sydney Opera House – all the way along to the eighteenth hole, the Statue of Liberty.

Jack tried not to let the score get to him. He took each shot carefully and deliberately. The crowd was busy working out the maths after every shot; none of the other players had caught up with the two leaders. The people flanking the course knew that it was between Caitlin and Jack. Jack tried to block them out. He pretended he was alone, playing the round early in the morning before anyone else was there. He played each hole for par.

At the Sydney Opera House, which was a complicated par four, Caitlin mishit. Her ball clanged against one of the shell-like roofs and bounced backwards. Jack was level with her score.

As they moved to the final Wonder, the Statue of Liberty, they were neck and neck.

Caitlin went first. Her shot rolled gently along the causeway on to Ellis Island, then slowed just inches from the green. She grinned at Jack and raised an eyebrow. She would putt the ball on her next go and would be one under par. She would win. Unless he did even better.

Jack gave his arms a gentle shake before placing the ball carefully on the tee. He closed his eyes for a moment and imagined the ball flying in exactly the right direction. He imagined himself putting £50 into the Paris fund.

He opened his eyes, took a few practice strokes, then hit the ball smartly in the centre.

The crowd held its breath as the ball flew right over the Atlantic Ocean.

It bounced once on the green.

It rolled towards the hole.

And dropped in.

The crowd roared!

A hole-in-one! He'd done it! Caitlin couldn't catch up now.

Jack felt slaps on his back. His hand was shaken again and again. And there was Lauren clapping and clapping. She picked him up and whirled him round. Jack hugged her back tightly. Then William, holding banknotes and grinning from ear to ear. Jack gripped the notes and they crackled in his hand. He felt light, as though he had a tiny bit of helium in his bones. He saw Caitlin smile as William gave her the second prize. Jack nodded at her; she gave a small wave back.

He'd won.

And the Paris fund was nearly halfway there.

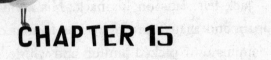

CHAPTER 15

When they got home Ruby was waiting for them on the doorstep, her doll's pram next to her. 'Where have you been?' she asked. 'Mum's worried. Did you see Dad? Did you go without me?'

Jack smiled at Ruby. Though she was cross, he could feel the bulge of cash in his back pocket. He'd won! And a tantrum from Ruby wasn't going to spoil it.

'Don't get your knickers in a twist,' Lauren said to Ruby. 'I brought you something. Close your eyes.'

Ruby screwed up her eyes so tightly that her eyelashes seemed to disappear.

'Hold out your hands.'

Ruby thrust her hands out, palms upwards. She had felt-tip marks all over her fingers.

Lauren reached into her pocket and lifted something out. She dropped it gently into Ruby's palm.

'Open your eyes.'

Ruby gasped.

So did Jack.

Ruby was holding a tiny glass horse – one of the ornaments they'd seen in Dad's bedroom.

'What do you say?' Lauren said.

'Thank you,' Ruby whispered. 'It's lovely. I'm going to call her Star, because she's all twinkly.' She had completed forgotten about being left behind.

Where had Lauren got that from?

Ruby held the little horse up to the sunlight. The pinkish glass glowed in her hands as the light shone through it. 'I'll look after it for ever,' she said. She went inside, carefully cradling it in her hands.

As soon as she was gone, Jack turned to Lauren. 'Where did that come from?' he said.

'Dad's,' Lauren said simply.

'I know that! I saw it there. But did Dad give it to you? Or . . . or –'

'Did I take it, you mean?' Lauren planted a hand heavily on her hip. 'What's it to you? It's just a stupid ornament.'

'But why?'

Lauren shrugged. 'Ruby liked it, didn't she? And no one will notice. And if they do, I'll say I broke it and was too scared to tell.'

93

Jack shook his head. 'You shouldn't have done it.' Somehow the money in his pocket didn't seem half as exciting any more.

'OK, fine, whatever,' Lauren said. 'Come on. We'd better let Mum know we're back. Are you ready for a telling-off?'

Jack nodded, then followed Lauren inside.

CHAPTER 16

'Where have you two been? You've been gone for hours.' Mum came out of the living room as soon as she heard their footsteps in the hall. She stood with her hands on her hips, the line between her eyebrows a deep furrow.

Jack looked down at his trainers.

'We went out for some air. We did say,' Lauren said.

'For five hours? I've been worried sick. I can't believe you'd be this irresponsible, Lauren. What am I supposed to think?'

Jack saw Lauren lift her head and tense a little. She was looking Mum straight in the eye.

'Well,' Lauren said, 'if you'd just let us go in the first place, then we wouldn't have had to sneak off. He's still our dad, you know.'

Mum's face was pale, even her lips looked as though

they were coated in ash. 'You've been with your dad? Even though I expressly said you weren't to go?'

Lauren shrugged.

'We just wanted to see him,' Jack whispered.

'Jack! I told you not to. It's too soon. I don't know what kind of place he's gone to. Is it suitable? I don't know anything about it.' Mum's voice wavered between angry and something else, something much sadder and deeper. She moved forward, as though she wanted to pull them both into a hug.

Lauren stepped backwards. 'You can't stop me. I'm not a kid any more.'

'Well, maybe you should stop behaving like one. Sometimes I really do know best, Lauren,' Mum snapped.

Lauren turned away and ran up the stairs. Jack heard the slam of her bedroom door.

Mum looked at him. 'Oh, Jack.'

He stepped closer and wrapped his arms round her waist. He could feel her ribs beneath his palms. She dropped her cheek down on to the top of his head and just leaned there for a while. 'Oh, Jack,' she whispered.

CHAPTER 17

The next morning, Jack was woken by the sound of scuffling outside his bedroom door. He tried to pull the duvet over his head and ignore it, but then the door opened.

Ruby bustled in, half pushing, half dragging Billy.

'I've had an idea,' she said proudly. 'Look.'

Jack rubbed his eyes. 'Morning, Ruby. What's your idea?'

'Look!'

She pushed Billy forward. He stumbled a few paces. He was finding it hard to walk, because Ruby had put a big sign round his neck.

'For Sale,' it said in blue felt-tip. '£100.'

'What's for sale?' Jack asked. He sat up.

Ruby tutted, copying the noise that Auntie Joyce made when she found a red sock in someone's white wash. 'Billy, of course!'

Billy nodded.

'We talked about it, didn't we, Billy?' Ruby said. 'Lots of people adopt children. I've seen adverts on the telly. People give a little bit of money every month and get photos and letters from the kids they've adopted. Well, we thought someone might want to give all that money in one go. And they'd get to keep Billy. There would be enough money in the Paris fund then. You don't mind, do you, Billy?'

Billy lifted the sign and stuck the corner of it in his mouth.

Jack looked at the crooked sign round Billy's neck. He looked at the eager smile on Ruby's face. And he started to laugh. He lay back down, chuckling into his pillow.

'Don't laugh! It's a good idea!' Ruby said crossly.

The bubbles of laughter rose up in Jack again, he couldn't help it. He was starting to get a stitch.

'Stop it!' Ruby said.

Jack gasped a few times. He wiped his eyes. 'Sorry.'

'It's not funny. It's a good idea.'

'No,' Jack said softly. 'We can't sell Billy.'

'But . . .' Ruby's forehead creased in worry. 'How else will we get enough money? How else will we get Dad to come back? We need them to go to Paris. You said so. Lauren said so. If we don't get the money, me and Billy won't see Dad again!'

'Is that what you think?' Jack asked.

'Yes,' Ruby whispered.

Jack pushed back his duvet, reached over and lifted the sign from Billy's neck. 'Well, you will see Dad again. Whether we get the money or not.'

'Mum said I couldn't.'

'She said you couldn't *yesterday*, not for ever.' Jack held Ruby's shoulders firmly. 'Ruby, it's going to be OK. We don't have to sell Billy.'

'Promise?'

Jack nodded slowly. 'I promise.'

CHAPTER 18

To: fulldinnerjacket@gmail.com
From: jack.dempsey23@hotmail.co.uk
Subject: Dad's gone

Dear Paul,

I hope you're are doing OK and training isn't too hard. Everything is weird here and not in a good way. Dad has gone to stay at The Larches, which is a bed and breakfast place. I don't know when he's coming back. Me and Lauren went to visit him yesterday. Ruby and Billy didn't come because Mum said no.

The house feels funny without Dad in it. Do you think he'll be OK by himself? Will he get lonely, do you think?

Do you know who Elvis Presley is? I googled him because of something Dad said. I watched a clip. Elvis was singing a song about being in love for ever with just one person. It was in black and white and he had weird sticky-up hair and a suit that looked a bit mouldy. But it was still a good song. Dad sang it to Mum once, you know.

Hey, guess what? I won a golf tournament. Top prize was £50! I wasn't sure I could do it, but I got a hole-in-one on the very last hole.

Love,

Jack

P.S. Please don't tell anyone, but Lauren stole an ornament from Dad's bed and breakfast. And she didn't seem sorry about it.

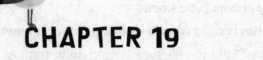

CHAPTER 19

Jack hit Send. He was glad that he'd told Paul about winning the tournament, but the person he really wanted to tell was Dad. Not that he could, because the trip to Paris was meant to be a surprise. But he wanted to so badly that it was like a pain in his stomach. He slipped out of his chair and went to the phone in the hall. There was a tattered old address book next to the phone. He looked up Dad's mobile number and dialled quickly. It went straight to voicemail. It was switched off.

Jack sat down on the bottom step and rested his chin on his hands. Dad usually switched his phone off on a Sunday morning, because he played golf then. But he wouldn't have gone there today, would he?

Would he?

Right.

'Mum! Mum, I'm going to see William,' Jack yelled. Then he left the house, not heading for the front but for the proper golf course, the grown-up course where Dad was a member.

It wasn't far, just beyond The Larches where Dad was staying. Jack put his hands in his pockets and walked quickly. He broke into a run.

Would Dad be playing golf today? What did it mean if he was? Jack tried to concentrate on his stride, the pounding of his feet on the pavement.

At the course, he turned left into the drive. There was a big white sign with royal blue paint advertising the golf course. Jack ran past it, up towards the clubhouse.

He stopped, panting, just outside Reception. He could see in through the window; some men were looking at the clubs that were on sale, a couple of women were trying on sun visors, the lady behind the desk was on the phone. Jack rested his hand on the door but didn't push it open.

He hadn't been here much before. Dad said he was still a bit too young to come and play, though he kept promising that Jack could come when he was older. Jack didn't know the name of the person at Reception. He didn't know any of the people waiting inside. He suddenly felt very shy, very small. He stepped back from the door.

He looked back down the drive. Maybe he should just go home. Or maybe he should go to the B and B to see if Dad was there. He looked up at the summer-blue sky.

'Jack?'

It was Dad's voice.

'Jack, what are you doing here?'

Jack froze. Dad was here. He *had* come golfing on the first weekend after moving out of the house. Jack felt sick, as though he'd accidentally drunk sour milk for breakfast.

'Jack?'

Jack turned slowly. Dad was walking towards him, pulling his golf bag behind him.

'What is it, Jack? Has something happened?'

Jack shook his head. 'I just wanted to see you.' He wished he could tell Dad about winning the Open. He wished Dad could smile and put his hand on his shoulder and say he was proud. Jack pressed his lips together.

'Oh, Jack.' Dad stepped forward. He pulled Jack into a loose hug. 'Does your mother know you're here?'

Jack shook his head, feeling the wool of Dad's jumper against his cheek.

Dad paused. 'Well, you can stay for a bit, but then I'll have to get you home. OK?'

'OK,' Jack whispered.

'Come on.' Dad rested his hand on Jack's shoulder and moved off. 'What shoes are you wearing?' He looked down at Jack's trainers and pulled a face. 'Oh, well. Just try not to let anyone see them.'

They headed off across the lawn in front of reception. The ground rose gently. To their left was a small lake with a fountain spraying into the air, the drops of water shining like tiny rainbows. On the right, the grass had been trimmed close as a squaddie's haircut. There were lots of holes close together to practise putting. It was just like William's World of Wonders, but without the Wonders.

'Where are we going?' Jack asked.

'Not far.'

They turned away from the teeing-off spot for the first hole. They were heading towards a copse of trees – Jack recognised oak and thought another might be willow. There was a kind of shed nestled in their shade. It looked a bit like a long bus shelter, except that one of the long sides was closed off by a net. There was no one else there.

'Driving practice,' Dad said. He rummaged in his bag until he found his tee-case, then pushed one into the ground a few metres away from the net.

Jack understood what the shed was for. Dad could wallop the ball as hard as he liked towards the back of the shed and the net would catch it. He could practise his swing without having to go and collect all the balls from miles away afterwards. Jack rested his hand on the open top of Dad's golf bag. 'Driver?' he asked.

'Three-iron, just to warm up,' Dad said.

Jack pulled the three-iron from the bag and handed it to Dad.

Dad lined up the club with the tee. He brought it down two or three times before connecting with the ball. The sound was loud, like a slap on flesh. The ball and the tee went flying, before landing dead in the netting.

Dad did it again. And again.

Jack crouched down on the ground. The sun was warm through his T-shirt. There were little flecks of grit in the dirt. He poked at them with his fingertip, arranging them into a pile like a tiny pyramid.

'Driver,' Dad said after a while.

Jack leaped up. The driver was a huge club with a head the size of a saucer. Jack pulled off the little sock that kept it clean and handed it to Dad.

He sat down on the grass again. Above him the breeze rustled the leaves of the trees in a gentle whisper. From far away, golfers shouted, 'Fore!' as their balls flew off in the wrong direction. No wonder Dad preferred here to home.

'OK,' Dad said after a while, 'your turn.'

Jack stood up. Dad lined the ball up for him, then handed him a lighter club. It was still way too big for him; he had to hold it just below the handle.

'There,' Dad said. 'Just hit it as hard as you can.'

Jack lifted the club, then brought it down – smack! – against the ball. The ball hooked left; if the net hadn't caught it he would have had to yell, 'Fore!'

'Try it again,' Dad said. 'Harder this time. Imagine it's something that's really annoyed you and smack it one.'

Jack thought. Something annoying. He thought of The Larches being Dad's new home.

This time, the ball went much further.

'Good!' Dad said.

Jack glared at the next ball. He thought of shouting and Ruby crying and slammed doors and silences. This time the ball spat up into the air and landed so hard in the net that Jack could see the dust being shaken from it.

'Well done!' Dad said, ruffling the top of Jack's hair.

'What do you think about?' Jack said. His voice sounded odd.

'What?' Dad asked.

'What do you think about when you hit the balls? Do you think of Mum?'

'Caroline?' Dad sounded confused. 'God, no. Of course not. I think about the bank manager, mostly. Or the overdraft. I think about smacking the overdraft into the middle of next week.'

Not Mum then. Did that mean that Dad wasn't angry with Mum? Did that mean that maybe he still liked her?

'Dad . . .' Jack paused as Dad teed up another ball. 'Dad, do you think you might come home soon?'

Dad looked at Jack, then sighed. 'I don't know. That's the honest truth. I'd like to, for you lot. But your mum and me, we don't see eye to eye about things any more.'

'But you want to come back, don't you?'

'Well,' Dad said slowly, 'I want to come back because I miss you guys. But is that enough? Maybe I shouldn't be telling you this, but here today, I've been trying to remember when me and your mum last made each other truly happy. And I can't remember. Before Billy was born? Maybe even before Ruby was born. And we've just lived with it. Being miserable. That's no way to be, is it?'

Jack felt numb. 'But what about us?' he whispered.

'I'll always be your dad. Always. Come on, I'd better get you back. Your mum will be worried.'

'Yes, she was yesterday, when me and Lauren got back.'

'Did you get a row?'

'A bit.' Jack bent down to collect some of the stray golf balls.

'Oh, Jack. That's not good. I know why you want to see me. I want to see you too. And Lauren, and Ruby and Billy. But you can't go upsetting your mum. It won't help matters.'

'Will you come in with me now?' Jack asked eagerly. 'Will you explain it? Talk to Mum?'

'Well, I'm not sure she wants to talk to me yet. I'll just walk with you to the end of the road. No point rushing things. I'll call her later.'

CHAPTER 20

That afternoon Jack was in his room, checking his emails, when the phone rang. Then he heard Mum's voice down in the hall. 'Hello?'

There was a pause.

'Gavin? Is that you?' Mum said.

Dad!

Jack got up from his chair slowly, so as not to make a noise. He moved to the door.

'Oh please, Gavin. I can't do this. Not now. No. No. Of course I won't stop you seeing the kids, but not till you're sorted out. I don't know when. They can't visit you there. You need to get a proper place, where they can stay. It isn't a proper place. You're not listening to me.'

Jack's fingers gripped the door handle hard; his knuckles turned white.

'No,' Mum's voice was angry now. 'Don't. Don't come over. Gavin! I don't want to see you. Nor do the kids.'

Jack's breath caught in his throat. He wanted to shout out to Mum, to tell her it wasn't true.

'Gavin. Leave it!' Mum shouted.

Jack heard the phone slam down. Then breathing – Mum breathing hard in the hallway.

He loosened his grip on the door. Should he go to her? Put his arm round her?

No.

She had told Dad that they didn't want him.

Jack felt a wave of anger hit him full in the chest. There was no way he was going to hug her, ever. He pushed the door to, hard. He threw himself down on the bed and punched the pillow with his fist, again and again and again. The duvet caught on his legs and twisted tight. He felt as though he was suffocating under the weight of air and feathers. He let himself fall against the pillow one last time. Then he lay still and the tears soaked into his pillowcase.

CHAPTER 21

Jack didn't know how long he lay there. He heard Ruby and Billy in the garden below, fighting over the swing. Ruby won. He heard Lauren come in from somewhere and turn her music on loud. It felt like a normal Sunday afternoon, except that his arms were too heavy to lift and the air was thick with feelings.

Then there was a different noise.

A key in the front door. 'Caro? Caroline?' Dad was here. In the house.

Jack heard Ruby scream in delight from the back garden.

He sat up in bed, listening.

Ruby was in the hall now, crying and laughing. Billy was with her too, whooping alongside her.

Dad laughed, saying their names over and over.

Jack opened his bedroom door and moved on to the landing. Lauren was there already. They both stood at the top of the stairs watching Ruby and Billy climb all over Dad at the bottom.

Mum came out of the sitting room. She looked pale and frightened.

'Caro?' Dad said. 'You can't keep them from me. You can't.'

'We talked about this.' Mum's voice shook. 'Ruby, Billy, go back to the garden!'

Mum tried to shoo Ruby away from Dad.

Jack realised he was holding his breath. He let it out slowly. He could feel a pulse behind his eyes that made him feel ill.

'Caro, this is not right!'

Then Jack couldn't make out the words, it was all yelling and anger and ugly. He sat down heavily on the top step. Lauren sat next to him. It was like looking down a dark well, where bad things twisted below. Ruby was crying now. Billy too. There was a bubble of snot on his upper lip. Mum was between Ruby and Dad; Ruby's arms clawed for him. Mum had tears on her face.

Ruby struggled against Mum's arm, trying to wriggle free. 'Daddy! My daddy!' she sobbed.

'Go,' Mum cried. 'Go, just go. Please?'

Dad seemed to crumple. He stepped towards the door.

'No!' Ruby yelled.

But Dad was already on the path, moving away fast.

'No!' Ruby threw herself forward. She slipped past Mum's arm. She was out the door. Running. She disappeared from Jack's view. Outside.

'Ruby!'

Mum's yell was drowned out by another noise.

The squeal of brakes in the street.

'Ruby!'

Jack had never heard a noise like the one Mum was making. High, desperate, terrified. A noise like the end of the world.

Mum ran out. Jack was up and running down the stairs, Lauren behind him, scooping up Billy as they passed.

There was a car outside their gate. A driver got out. 'I didn't see her,' he whispered. 'I didn't see her.'

Jack stopped next to the car.

Ruby lay on the tarmac, small and soft and still. Her leg was twisted underneath her in the wrong shape.

Dad dropped beside her; he said her name over and over.

Jack watched. There was a thought, somewhere far away but getting closer. He knew there was something he should do, but he couldn't think what it was. It was as though his brain had powered down. He shook his head violently. What should he do?

Ambulance.

The word was like a switch, bringing the world back into focus. His mind leaped into action, his legs too. He ran back inside. To the phone. He picked it up. His fingers fumbled over the buttons, but then he dialled 999.

'Emergency. Which service, please?'

'What? Hello, my sister. She's hurt. She's been hit by a car.'

'Ambulance. Putting you through.'

The line changed tone, then another person spoke. 'Ambulance. State your emergency,' someone said.

'My sister. Please come quickly.'

'What's happened to her?'

'She's been hit by a car.'

'OK. Where is she?'

Jack gave his address quickly.

'The ambulance is on its way. Are you with your sister now? Is she breathing?'

'No. I mean, I don't know. She's outside.'

'Do you have a mobile I can call you back on?' the voice asked.

'No.'

'Is there a grown-up with you?'

'Mum and Dad.'

'OK. Here's what you need to do. Go back outside. Tell them the ambulance is coming. If either of them has a mobile, ask them to call 999 and ask for CPR instruction. That's CPR instruction. Have you got that?'

'CPR. Yes.'

'Good lad.'

Jack hung up and ran back outside. Mum was still making that awful, awful noise that made him feel sick deep inside. Dad was kneeling next to Ruby.

'Mum, Dad, the ambulance is coming,' Jack said. 'They said call 999 and ask for CPR instruction. Is she breathing?'

Dad looked up. His eyes didn't really seem to see Jack. He didn't move.

'Is she breathing?' Jack shouted.

Just then, he heard the wail of the ambulance. It was close by. He felt his legs go weak underneath him. He sat down heavily on the curb.

The ambulance pulled up beside them, its lights flashing, even as the people in green jumpsuits rushed out.

Jack saw them speaking to Mum, moving her aside. There was a stretcher with a bright red blanket. Dad tried to stand. There was a policeman too. The driver was talking to him.

And Ruby. Lying still and white.

Lauren was beside him, with Billy in her arms. Her face was as drained as Ruby's.

Then Ruby was in the ambulance, with Mum and Dad next to her.

'Lauren, look after the others,' Mum shouted. 'I'll call from the hospital.'

Lauren nodded.

The ambulance was gone, blue lights and noise moving further and further away.

Jack watched it go from the curb. He couldn't move. Lauren tucked one hand under his elbow and yanked him to his feet. 'Come on,' she said. 'Come on.'

CHAPTER 22

Inside the house, Lauren took charge.

'Sit down, Billy; you too, Jack,' she said pointing to the kitchen table. 'It's going to be OK. Everything is going to be OK. I know, I'll make us hot chocolate.'

Jack nodded. It was what Paul used to do when he looked after them. As soon as Mum and Dad went out, he'd make hot chocolate. Then they'd rearrange the furniture in the living room to make a den and sit and play cards until Billy or Ruby fell asleep where they were. Hot chocolate was a good idea. 'Thanks,' he whispered.

Lauren flicked on the kettle and emptied two sachets into cups and a third into Billy's plastic beaker with a spout. She put cold milk into Billy's beaker and hot water into the cups.

When she put his cup down, Jack wrapped his icy cold fingers round it and just sniffed at the steam coming off it.

Lauren sat too. Billy climbed down from the chair and toddled towards the back door with his beaker of chocolate milk. *Does he even know what's happening?* Jack wondered. Billy sat down heavily with his back against the door and sipped his drink.

'Will Ruby be all right?' Jack asked Lauren.

'Yes. Maybe. Oh, I don't know.'

They sat and finished their drinks, waiting for the phone to ring. Jack asked if they could try ringing Dad's mobile, but Lauren said no; it was better just to wait. So they waited.

And waited.

It felt like they'd been sitting still for weeks, but it was maybe only an hour, when Jack heard the front door open. He pushed his chair back and ran to the hall, 'Mum!'

'No, sweetheart. It's just me,' Auntie Joyce said. 'Caro called me and asked me to come. Wait while I get my coat off and the kettle on, then I can tell you what I know.'

Once Auntie Joyce had her tea in front of her, she sighed. 'Ruby's in surgery,' she said.

'She's alive?' The relief in Jack's voice was clear for everyone to hear.

Auntie Joyce's eyes widened. 'Oh, honey pie. Of course she's alive! Did you not know that? I'm sorry. I should have raced round here to tell you.' Auntie Joyce leaned forward and kissed the top of Jack's head. Normally he would have hated that, but today it felt nice.

'She's alive.' Auntie Joyce paused. 'But she's not well. She has internal injuries. That's what they said. I don't really know what. I mean, there's a lot inside you that can go wrong, isn't there? But they are trying to fix it.'

'How long before we know?' Lauren asked.

'Hours, I think,' Auntie Joyce said. 'She'll be in surgery for a while and then it will take a bit longer for her to wake up.' Auntie Joyce stood up and went over to the sink. She rinsed her cup under the tap and left it to drain. 'You kids should just get on with things until we know.'

'Can't we wait at the hospital?' Jack asked.

'Sorry, sweetheart. No visitors for a while, just your mum and dad. What would you normally do now? Play on your computer? Go outside? We could walk down to adventure golf if you like.'

'No!' Jack said. 'We need to stay in the house, in case anyone phones.'

'Sure, sure,' Auntie Joyce said. 'Good point. We'll stay in, then. What would you like to do?'

Jack looked at Lauren. She had pulled her hair around to the front of her face and was busy making lots of small plaits with it. Her eyes were fixed on the tight strands. Billy had found a toy car under the fridge; he was driving it in a circle between his legs.

'We could make a den,' Jack suggested.

Lauren glanced over at him.

'A den?' Auntie Joyce asked.

'Yes. Like Paul used to. In the living room. We get blankets and duvets and things and push the sofas together. We build a den. And, I don't know, we sit in it.'

Lauren nodded slowly.

That was all Auntie Joyce needed. 'Up,' she said. 'Up, go and get the things, the duvets. Chop-chop.'

Jack felt a small flicker of excitement. Lauren gave him a watery smile. Then they were up and out of the kitchen. Jack ran upstairs, Billy trotting close behind him. In his bedroom, Jack whipped the duvet off his bed and slung it over his shoulder. He threw a pillow at Billy. 'Catch!'

Then he went into Mum and Dad's room –

Mum's room; it was just Mum and Billy's room now.

He went into Mum's room and took her big duvet too. With both duvets balanced on his shoulders he was like a big, walking ice-cream cone. Billy climbed up on to the chair next to his cot and tugged his crochet blanket out through the bars. Teddy Volvo rolled out from it, so Billy reached through and grabbed him too.

Jack heard Lauren tramping back downstairs, so he followed her.

In the living room, Auntie Joyce had drawn the curtains. The room was dark, with a rectangle of light falling into it from the hallway.

'Push the sofa,' Lauren said.

Jack dropped his bundle, then helped Lauren shunt the sofa around, so that it had its back to the room. It was a tight squeeze, but they just did it. The sofa opposite wouldn't spin round, it was too heavy. Instead, they just wiggled it closer to the first one. Billy jumped up on to it. He buried his head in a cushion and stuck his bum up in the air. He might have been giggling, he might have been crying – Jack wasn't sure.

'Move over, Billy,' Lauren said. 'Incoming duvet.'

She threw Mum's duvet up so that it landed over the backs of both sofas. Now there was a little dark cave in the middle of the living room. Jack pushed his own duvet inside, to make the floor. Lauren added her own bedding to the roof, so the duvets hung down low on all sides.

They crawled inside.

Jack could make out Lauren and Billy's shapes, but he couldn't see their faces – it was too dark. He held himself still and listened to their breathing. Billy sounded a bit snotty.

'Lauren,' Jack whispered.

'Yes?'

'Is it going to be all right?'

Lauren didn't answer. Jack heard the creak of the sofa as she leaned back against it. Billy curled up on the floor and rested his head against Jack's leg. Jack sighed. He dropped his hand on to Billy's head and stroked his hair.

Then he felt Lauren's hand reach out. They bumped fingers and Lauren slid her hand round his, holding it tight. Jack smiled in the darkness.

'Paul had a torch. Do you remember?' Lauren said softly. 'He kept it on his key ring. It was only little, but it was enough for us to see by; just enough to be able to see the cards in your hand.'

Jack nodded. Lauren must have sensed the movement, because she gave his hand another squeeze.

'It's all you need, a little light like that. It's all you need.'

She let go of his hand and curled around, pulling Billy in close. Jack lay down too and let the warm duvet cradle him.

CHAPTER 23

Auntie Joyce took them to the hospital the next morning. Mum had stayed overnight with Ruby. Auntie Joyce led them down corridors painted lavender blue. The sunlight tumbled in through the windows, so they walked through patches of warm air and glitter-dust.

But Jack shivered.

Was Ruby OK? Was she hooked up to machines? Covered in bandages? Was she going to die?

Auntie Joyce put her arm round him and pulled him closer.

They followed the signs to the children's ward – Paediatrics. Jack could tell they were getting close, because the decoration changed. The blue walls changed to sunshine yellow, with pictures of cartoon characters on them.

Auntie Joyce led them through a set of double doors. Beyond the doors was the children's ward. Jack flashed a glance around. *Where was Ruby?* Some of the beds had children in them, playing games or sleeping. Others were empty as their owners rampaged down the central space. It sounded a lot like a school playground, with yelps and laughs and the odd cry. The smell reminded Jack of scraped knees, plasters and disinfectant.

There was no sign of Ruby.

A nurse smiled at Auntie Joyce, then pointed them in the right direction. They walked away from the noise, towards one of the rooms at the end of the ward. The door was closed.

A man was sitting outside the door with his head in his hands.

Lauren stopped walking. 'Dad?'

Dad looked up. His eyes were red and his skin was the colour of old chewing gum. He tried to smile, but the light didn't reach his eyes.

Lauren ran past Jack, towards Dad. 'Dad? How's Ruby?'

Dad stood up and hugged Lauren. He blinked a few times. 'She's doing fine. She woke up for a while. She said a few words. Doctors say she'll be OK.'

He dropped back on to his seat with a sigh. Billy climbed up on to his lap and turned his face into Dad's shirt.

Auntie Joyce spoke. 'And Caro? How's she?'

'I don't know,' Dad said. 'She's angry. She won't even speak to me.'

Auntie Joyce patted Dad's shoulder. 'Why don't you go back to the B and B? You look tired,' she said. 'I can call you if there's any news.'

Lauren turned in confusion. 'But he should wait. He should –'

'No, love,' Dad interrupted. 'Joyce is right. I've been out here too long. Your mother . . . well, she doesn't need me here right now.'

'But Ruby does!' Lauren said fiercely.

Dad ignored Lauren. He looked at Auntie Joyce. 'She can't keep me out for ever. Speak to her, would you? And tell her . . .' he paused. 'Tell her to get some sleep too.'

Dad lowered Billy off his lap on to the ground, then he stood up. He moved away from them without look-ing back. He was gone.

Auntie Joyce shook her head. Then she pushed open the door.

Ruby lay in a bed that looked five times too big for her. Her eyes were closed and her face was blotchy red and white. A clear plastic bag full of liquid hung next to her bed with a tube leading from it to a needle in the back of her hand.

126

Mum sat next to her. She looked up and smiled at them. 'Hi, guys,' she said quietly. 'Come in.' She got up out of the chair, wincing as she moved towards them. She must have been sitting still for ages. Mum gave everyone a short, tight hug. Jack took a few steps towards the bed.

'How's Ruby?' he whispered.

'She's asleep,' Mum said. 'Has been for hours.'

'When can she come home?'

Mum frowned. 'I don't know. She has to heal properly and they need to make sure she doesn't have an infection. A week, maybe.'

'You need a break,' Auntie Joyce said. 'Come and have a cup of tea with me. There's a canteen here somewhere.'

'But what if she wakes up?'

'Jack and Lauren will stay, won't you?' Auntie Joyce asked. 'One of them can come and get you if Ruby needs you. Come on, you look exhausted.'

Mum looked at the bed. Her face was a map of lines as she frowned. Then she nodded quickly. She scooped Billy up and followed Auntie Joyce out of the room.

There was a silence. Only the far-off sounds of the children's ward reminded them that there were other people in the world.

Lauren sat in the chair that Mum had been in, right up close to the bed. Jack looked around and pulled up another hard plastic chair. Ruby lay still; she reminded him of those statues that lie on top of coffins in the cathedral, but more blotchy.

'She looks OK, doesn't she?' he said. 'Do you think they had to stitch her up?'

'She had surgery. Of course they had to stitch her up, otherwise her insides would fall out.'

'Do you reckon she's all bandaged then? Under the blanket?'

Lauren scowled. 'We are not going looking for her scars while she's knocked out. We'll wait until she's awake at least.'

'Is she in a coma?' Jack asked.

'No. No, she isn't. She's just asleep.'

They sat side by side, watching the tiny little movement of the sheet as Ruby breathed in and out. Jack pulled his foot up on to the chair and started playing with his laces. He undid the knot, then did it up again, tighter.

Then Lauren's elbow jabbed his side. 'Look!' she said.

Ruby's eyelids flickered, flinched. Then, slowly, her eyes opened.

She smiled at them both. 'Hey.'

'Hey, yourself,' Jack said. He was surprised to realise that his eyes were prickling with tears.

'Does it hurt? Do you need a doctor?' Lauren asked.

Ruby thought for a minute. 'No,' she said. 'Well, it hurts a bit. What happened? Where's Mum and Dad?'

'Mum's having a cup of tea with Auntie Joyce. She's been here all night. Dad just left.'

'He left?' Ruby's voice was weak and croaky, but she still managed to sound hurt.

Lauren nodded. 'He was sent home really. Auntie Joyce said it was better for him to wait at the B and B.'

'Why?'

The question hung in the air between them. Jack shuffled his chair closer to the bed. 'What do you remember?' he asked.

Ruby frowned. 'Dad was home. And then he was leaving again. And then, there was a big noise and my leg hurt and my tummy, and then I was asleep.'

'A car hit you,' Lauren said simply. 'A car hit you and you came to hospital.'

'So why isn't Dad here?' The last word was more of a choked sob.

Jack flashed a look at Lauren.

Lauren sighed. 'Don't get upset. Do you want a drink of water or something? Shall I get Mum?'

'I want my daddy,' Ruby whispered.

129

Lauren frowned, then reached out and stroked Ruby's face. 'Listen. He was here, but he had to go. Mum's cross with him.'

'Why?'

'I don't know.' Lauren sighed. 'Maybe she thinks that if Dad hadn't come to the house then you wouldn't be in hospital. Who knows what they're thinking.'

'But,' Ruby whispered, 'that isn't fair. I didn't look before I crossed the road. That isn't Dad's fault.'

'Don't worry,' Lauren said. 'Really, don't worry. You just need to get better. You're going to be OK. It's good, it's all good. Don't cry.'

'But I've made it worse.' Ruby's voice was so quiet, Jack could hardly hear her. 'Now Dad will never come home. And it's my fault.' She pulled the sheet up over her face.

'We'll fix it,' Jack said. 'Please don't cry.' He stroked the top of her head where her brown curls spread across the pillow.

Ruby quietened slowly. Jack eased the sheet down off her face. She looked grey and tired. Her eyelids drooped, then closed. She was asleep again.

'Well done,' Lauren said sarcastically.

'What?'

'Why did you tell her you'd fix it? How exactly do you plan on fixing it? Mum's going to be furious with Dad over this.'

Jack had a horrible feeling that Lauren was right, but he refused to admit it. He had said he'd make it right and he would. 'We have to make it all right. For Ruby. And for us. And for Mum and Dad.'

'They're not even talking to each other.'

'That's exactly why we need to do something. We've already got some of the money we need to get them to Paris. How far would ninety pounds get them?'

'Somewhere in Kent, probably. Jack, how can we get them to Paris when we can't even get them in the same room?'

'They are *not* going to turn down a free holiday. They're cross with each other, they're not *mental*.'

'Aren't they?' Lauren said bitterly. 'They seem pretty mental to me.'

Jack frowned. Lauren had a point.

CHAPTER 24

To: <u>fulldinnerjacket@gmail.com</u>
From: <u>jack.dempsey23@hotmail.co.uk</u>
Subject: Ruby's on the mend

Dear Paul,

I thought you might like to know, Ruby is definitely on the mend. Today, when we went in, she was eating ice cream and watching cartoons on a little telly in her room. She says that except for the needles, it's a bit like being on holiday.

I hope she can come home soon.

Mum and Dad still aren't talking. Well, Mum isn't anyway. Dad goes to the hospital at different visiting times to Mum. The head nurse understands. Her name is Pamela and her mum and dad are divorced, even though they are really old. She gave me orange juice last time we were there and told me that when she got married, her mum and dad had to sit at different tables at the wedding to stop them arguing. She lets Dad visit Ruby even though it isn't officially visiting time, so that he can avoid Mum.

When Ruby's well enough to walk around by herself, she'll come home. That's what Pamela says anyway. I hope it's soon.

Love,

Jack

To: jack.dempsey23@hotmail.co.uk
From: fulldinnerjacket@gmail.com
Subject: RE: Ruby's on the mend

Dear Jack,

Why are soldiers so handy?

Because they're in the army!

Handy, army? Get it? Ooh, you're a tough crowd.

That's absolutely blinding news about Ruby. Nice one. I always knew she was tough as old boots. She'll be back home getting on your nerves and making you play daft games in no time, you'll see.

Well done on winning the inaugural William's World of Wonders Open Tournament. I always knew you were a mini Tiger Woods. I'm not getting in a lot of golf here, but I have been practising my running around and climbing things. I finished the assault course today. I won't tell you my time, because you won't be impressed. But I finished it! First time I've actually managed to get the whole way round without being sick. Go Team Me!

I'm sorry to hear your mum and dad are still fighting. As far as your mum goes, well, she's angry. There's no talking to people when they're angry. We had a lecture on effective negotiating last week. They told us that if the person you're negotiating with loses their temper, then they can't hear you any more. It's like something in their brain switches off. There's no point trying to win hearts and minds when you're in the middle of a battle.

Love,

Paul

To: fulldinnerjacket@gmail.co.uk
From: jack.dempsey23@hotmail.com
Subject: Hearts and minds?

Dear Paul,

What does hearts and minds mean?

Love,

Jack

To: <u>jack.dempsey23@hotmail.co.uk</u>
From: <u>fulldinnerjacket@gmail.com</u>
Subject: RE: Hearts and minds?

Dear Jack,

There are two sides to a person, their heart and their mind. Or, to put it another way, emotions and logic. When someone is angry, then they're all emotion, no logic. There's just no room inside for their brain to say, 'Hang on there a minute.' There's no point negotiating with angry people. You just have to wait for them to calm down.

You have to be patient with your mum and dad.

Love,

Paul

CHAPTER 25

Jack logged out of his email. Hearts and minds. Was it true that Mum and Dad were too busy being angry to feel anything else? He thought it might be.

He stood up. He had been at his desk too long. The house was quiet. He wandered out of his room, vaguely looking for Lauren or Billy. Or maybe even Mum.

He found Lauren out in the garden. She was sunbathing. She was wearing her swimming costume and lying back on a sunlounger. Billy was curled up on the grass, fast asleep. The air felt hot and heavy as a duvet. Jack thought it must be nice to just curl up in it and sleep, without a care in the world.

'Where's Mum?' Jack asked.

'Cleaning the bathroom.'

'Why?'

'I don't know. Go and get me an ice lolly, would you?'

'OK.'

Inside, at the freezer, Jack suddenly wondered whether Mum would like one too.

Jack went to find her. He pushed open the bath-room door. Mum was leaning into the bath, scrubbing at the sides. The smell of the cleaning stuff made Jack cough. Mum looked up, then sat back on her heels. She wiped a strand of hair out of her eyes with the back of her arm. She looked hot and cross.

'Hi, Mum,' Jack said.

'What, Jack? I'm busy.'

'Why?'

'Why what?' Mum said.

'Why are you busy? We're out in the garden. You could come and play. We're going to have ice lollies.' Jack wasn't sure what he meant. It just seemed wrong that Mum should be inside on a nice day when she could be out with them.

'I haven't got time to play. I need to get the house straight. It needs to be nice for when . . .' Mum stopped, her voice sounded shaky. She took a breath. 'It needs to be nice for when Ruby gets home.'

'Ruby doesn't notice the cleaning,' Jack said.

'Well, *I* notice. And I want it to be nice for her.'

'When is she coming home?' Jack asked.

137

Mum looked away, then reached back into the bath to carry on scrubbing. 'Soon,' she said. 'Soon.'

Back in the garden, Jack handed Lauren an ice lolly. She bit off the plastic wrapping and crunched into the lolly.

'Come to the beach,' Jack said.

Lauren sighed and shuffled lower on the sunlounger. 'I'm busy.'

'No, you're not. You're just lying there going red.'

Lauren sat up quickly and held out her arms. They were the soft brown of caramel. 'No, I'm not!' she said.

'Yes, you are,' Jack grinned. 'Like a lobster. Like a pillar box. Like a London bus. Ruby red!'

He stopped. Ruby's name seemed to hang in the air between them.

Lauren sighed. 'OK.' She stood up. 'Let's go to the front.'

'What about Billy?' Jack looked down. Billy was still fast asleep in the shade.

Lauren scooped Billy up. He murmured, but didn't wake. 'He's having an afternoon nap. I'll put him in Mum's bed. I'll be right down.'

Jack followed her through the house. He waited at the bottom of the stairs while Lauren tucked Billy in then scrambled into her jeans and T-shirt. Lauren shouted goodbye to Mum then came down.

138

Outside, Jack took long strides towards the beach. It felt good to be doing something normal. It felt as if too much of their life was spent waiting and watching.

He broke into a trot.

'Hey, wait for me!' Lauren yelled behind him.

But he didn't slow down. As he ran, his face broke into a smile. He raced past the tourists with their sun hats and ice creams; he ignored the slow-loping horses and the swooping seagulls. In a moment, he was at the adventure golf.

'It's the Champ!' William gave him a wave. 'Four under today? What do you reckon?'

Jack grinned. 'Five.'

'We need to think about the autumn repairs soon. The Statue of Liberty has lost one of the spikes off her crown. Some hooligan smashed a ball straight at her. I know he was only a toddler, but that's no excuse for a bad shot.' William disappeared into the wooden shed at the side of the course. He reappeared quickly with Jack's favourite putter. 'And the Leaning Tower of Pisa is looking a bit too wonky.'

Jack nodded, then picked out a ball and set off for the first hole. Lauren sat on her favourite bench, looking out at the navy blue sea.

Jack lined his ball up on the tee and positioned himself for the shot. The fixed pump on the Niagara

Falls meant that water rushed fiercely between him and the hole. He took the holes slowly and methodically. He wasn't after an impressive score today – he just wanted to be here in the sunshine, putting balls.

After about twenty minutes, he noticed Lauren had moved off her bench and was standing by the side of the green.

'Jack,' she said, 'I'm going to the grabber machine.'

'Why?' he asked.

'To see if I can do any better than Ruby. Lend me 20p?'

'We should really put all our money in the Paris fund,' he said.

Lauren shrugged, 'Twenty pence won't make a difference. Just lend me the money, would you?'

Jack felt around in his pocket. He had a few coins in there. He thought about the jar at home, half-full. There was nearly enough money for one ticket to Paris in there, but one wasn't enough. 'It should go in the jar. No one ever wins on the grabber anyway.'

'Come on, Jack. Don't be mean.'

'No.'

Lauren frowned. 'It's just 20p. And I can spend it winning something for Ruby instead of putting it in a jar that's never going to have enough money in it.'

'Yes it will!'

'And even if it does – which it won't – Mum and Dad aren't talking to each other! They hate each other. Sending them to Paris won't make a blind bit of difference.'

'Yes it will!' Jack felt his eyes sting.

'Don't start crying!' Lauren snapped. 'I'm only telling you the truth. Grow up, Jack!'

Jack felt a flame of anger burst into life inside him. He wiped his eyes. 'I'm not crying. And they will go to Paris. We just need to be patient, Paul says. We need to wait for them to calm down.'

'And then what? They shake little fingers and say sorry? Well, they won't. Dad's gone and he isn't coming back.'

'He hasn't gone! He's just up the road.'

Lauren shook her head. 'He's gone and he isn't coming back and you have to get used to it.' She spat out the words, then spun round on her heel. She stalked away, heading out of the course.

Jack let his club fall against the Taj Mahal. He pulled a twenty-pence piece from his pocket. Should he have given it to Lauren? Or should it go in the Paris fund with the money he'd won and the rest of their coins? Was there really no point? He shook his head angrily. Lauren was wrong – he was sure she was wrong.

He sat down on the edge of the green. The twenty pence lay in his palm. On one side was the queen's profile. He flipped it over. On the other side was a rose, its petals opening up to the sun, and above it, a crown. Flowers and Crowns. Hearts and Minds.

He would toss for it.

Heads, he would put it in the Paris fund.

Tails, he would give it to Lauren.

He flipped the coin high into the air, caught it and slapped it on to the back of his hand.

He uncovered it slowly.

Tails.

Tails?

Jack looked out towards the beach. There were families there, building sandcastles, eating ice creams, playing games. He looked away.

There was no sign of Lauren.

He would spend the money on the grabber machine, like Lauren said. If he was giving up, then at least he could try and get something for Ruby while he was at it.

He handed his club and ball back to William. He didn't bother replying to William's questions about scores and holes. He just waved and turned away.

He walked along the front until he reached the arcade. He could feel the heat off the ground through the soles of his shoes; it was as though the whole place was burning. At the grabber machine he dropped in the twenty pence into the slot. The lights at the sides of the machine flashed into life; two buttons, forward and sideways, glowed green. He hit the first button carelessly, then thumped the other.

The grabbing arm moved forward over the pile of teddies. It shuddered to the right. It dropped down with its claws open. Then the metal claws closed. They closed . . . right round the head of a pink teddy!

Jack froze.

The arm rose up again, carrying the teddy with it. All the way back to the start. And the teddy didn't fall, didn't wobble, didn't drop.

The claws opened slowly, letting the teddy fall into the wire tray by Jack's knees.

He had won.

No one ever won.

But he had.

He reached in and lifted the teddy free.

Its pink fur was soft and fluffy. It was smiling and its eyes were open wide. Ruby was going to love it. Well, she was going to love it so long as she didn't mind that it was Jack, and not her, who had won it.

As Jack walked home, he cradled the bear in the crook of his elbow. Was winning the teddy a sign? Had he been right not to put the money in the Paris fund? He didn't want to believe it, but maybe Lauren was right.

CHAPTER 26

Mum had finished cleaning the bathroom when he got in. She was sitting at the kitchen table with her hands wrapped round a cup of tea. There was no sign of Billy. He must still be asleep.

'Hello, love,' she said softly. 'Did you have a nice time?' She reached out and pulled him into a hug.

Jack nodded and held up the teddy bear. 'I won this for Ruby,' he said.

'Oh, that's nice. She'll like that. Listen, I'm sorry about before. I didn't mean to snap at you.'

Jack shrugged. It didn't matter now.

'Where's Lauren? We need to go to the hospital in a bit.'

'I don't know. We had a fight.'

'Oh, Jack. What about?'

Jack pulled away from Mum's arm and sat down

opposite. He stood the bear up on its back legs and made it do a little dance.

Mum frowned. 'This is all hard for you, isn't it?'

Jack pirouetted the bear.

'It's for the best though,' Mum continued. 'I know it doesn't feel like it now, but you'll see. When you're a bit older, you'll understand.'

What? Jack opened his mouth to argue, but just at that moment, the phone rang.

Mum pushed aside her cup and stood up.

Jack heard her speaking from the hallway.

'Yes, speaking. She did what? Where is she? Yes. Of course. No, I'll be there. No, don't do that. I'll be there.'

Mum stormed back into the kitchen, her lips pressed together in fury.

'Mum?' Jack asked. 'Mum, what is it?'

'Lauren! She's been arrested!'

Jack gasped. 'Arrested?'

'Well,' Mum was pulling on her cardigan and pushing her feet into her trainers, 'not arrested. Held. At the chemist. They say she was stealing lipsticks. I have to go.' Mum looked at Jack straight in the eye. 'Lauren wouldn't do something like that, would she?'

Jack couldn't answer. He felt his face flush red.

Mum groaned. 'Oh, Jack, what's happening?'

Jack concentrated hard on the pink bear.

Mum put her hand on his shoulder and squeezed. 'I won't be long. Wake Billy, will you? And take him to the launderette. Wait there with Joyce till I get back.'

Jack nodded.

Then Mum was running out of the front door.

Jack was left alone.

He thought about going upstairs to wake Billy. He knew that was what he should do. He went up the first step, then the second. Then he stopped. That wasn't what he wanted to do at all. What he wanted was Dad.

He jumped down back into the hallway. He opened the address book and found Dad's mobile number. The phone rang a few times, then clicked into Voicemail. Jack reached for the Yellow Pages from the cupboard under the phone. He looked up Bed & Breakfast. There! There was Dad's one. He dialled the number.

'Hello, The Larches,' a raspy woman's voice said.

'Hello, I need to speak to my dad. Gavin. Gavin Dempsey. Please,' Jack added.

'OK, I think he's in. Hold on.'

Jack heard the clatter of the receiver being dropped on to a desk. Then he heard the woman yell, 'Gav! Gav! Phone!'

There was a long wait. Then Jack heard his dad's voice. He felt a sudden rush of warmth and longing at the same time.

'Hello,' Dad said.

'Dad.' Jack couldn't manage any more.

'Jack? Is that you? What is it? Has something happened to Ruby?'

'No,' Jack said quickly, 'she's fine. It's Lauren. Oh, Dad, she's been stealing things from shops. She got caught. Mum's gone there now to get her out. But me and Billy are on our own. Can you come? Please?'

'What about your Auntie Joyce?'

'What about her?'

There was a pause on the other end of the line. The plastic handset felt slippery in Jack's hand – his palms were sweating.

'Jack, pal, I can't just come over. Your mum would have a fit and she's already got enough on her plate. It might be better if you called Joyce.'

'But Dad, I want you to come!'

'I can't, son. It's not that I don't want to, but it would be like pouring petrol on the fire.'

'But what about Lauren? Aren't you cross with her? Don't you want to come and tell her off?'

'I expect your mother is doing enough of that for

the both of us. Maybe what Lauren needs is for me to listen when all the drama has blown over.'

Jack couldn't reply. It felt as though Dad were a hundred miles away, not just round the corner. And he wasn't coming any closer.

He heard a noise behind him. He looked round. Billy stood about halfway down the stairs, dragging Teddy Volvo behind him.

'Billy's awake,' Jack said.

'Good. Do you want me to call Joyce for you?'

Jack shook his head, then remembered that Dad couldn't see. 'No,' he said. 'We'll be OK.'

'OK, then. Bye, Jack.'

'Bye, Dad.'

Jack dropped the phone gently back into the cradle. Dad wasn't going to help. He stared at the phone for a second. Things were getting worse, not better, whatever Mum said.

He turned to look at Billy. 'You know something, Billy? I think it's about time that we did some of the deciding, don't you?'

Billy lifted Teddy Volvo and began chewing on his ear.

'Exactly,' Jack said.

CHAPTER 27

Mum and Lauren came home about an hour later. Jack had spent the time thinking and thinking. Now he was waiting by the front window, impatient to see Lauren. They wouldn't send her to prison, would they? Billy sat in the middle of the floor watching the telly.

Finally they walked up the front path, Lauren in front, her head hanging down. Mum walked behind. Jack could see her mouth moving nineteen to the dozen, but he couldn't hear what she was saying until Lauren opened the front door.

'. . . whole life been so ashamed. I can't believe it of you. A daughter of mine. Well, you can forget about going out on your own. Grounded until I can trust you again.'

Jack stepped carefully into the hallway.

'Jack?' Mum's furious eyes turned to him. 'Why aren't you at the launderette? I told you to wait there for me!'

Jack shrugged, but Mum's attention didn't stay on him for more than a second or two. 'Lauren, you go up to your room and you stay there until I tell you different!'

Lauren didn't need telling twice. She ran up the stairs. Jack heard her give a strangled sob. Then her door closed.

'I'm losing my grip,' Mum muttered, then walked into the kitchen. Jack heard her switch on the kettle.

Jack paused at the bottom of the stairs. Then he took a deep breath. He needed to speak to Lauren. Enough was enough.

He climbed up and knocked on her bedroom door.

She didn't answer.

He knocked again. Then, when there was still no reply, he opened it.

'What?' Lauren yelled.

Jack stepped into the room and closed the door behind him.

Lauren was lying face down on her bed. She twisted her head round to glare at him, her eyes bright and shining. 'What do you want?' she said.

'We need to do something. Things can't carry on

150

like this. No one speaking to anyone, everything feeling so horrible.'

'Well, it isn't my fault!' she said.

Jack paused. He didn't want to tell her that some of it was. He didn't want to make her angry. But she had been caught stealing, after all. That was her fault.

'Doesn't matter whose fault it is,' Jack said. 'The facts of it are, Mum and Dad can't even be in the same room together any more. How will Dad ever come home if things stay like this?'

'He isn't going to come home,' Lauren said simply.

'Don't!' Jack said. 'Don't say that.'

Lauren looked as though she was making up her mind. Would she argue or would she listen? Perhaps there had been enough fighting today because she raised herself up slowly and nodded. 'Fine. What were you thinking?'

Jack took a deep breath. 'We need to get them together, somewhere outside the house. Neutral ground. For negotiations to take place.'

'Have you been talking to Paul?'

'Maybe. He says they need to stop being angry before they can listen to each other. They need to be able to use their hearts and minds together. That's the way they do it in the army.'

'This isn't a war!' Lauren said hotly.

'Isn't it?' Jack said. 'It feels like it might be some-times. And we're the collateral damage. Well, I say it stops. You and me, we're like the United Nations in this house. We're going to set up a peace treaty.'

'How are we going to do that?'

Jack shook his head. 'I thought you might know. You're the eldest.'

Lauren flung herself back down on the bed and sighed.

'Come on, Lauren, you must have some ideas.'

'I came up with the Paris idea, didn't I? It was from my magazine. But we didn't get enough money and now it's too late.'

'Well, maybe we could find a cheaper Paris.'

Lauren snorted.

But Jack didn't reply.

He was thinking.

He knew where they could find Paris and it wouldn't cost them hundreds of pounds.

'There is a Paris,' Jack whispered. 'Right close by.'

'What do you mean?'

'There's an Eiffel Tower here. They don't have to go all the way to France.'

Lauren stared at him, trying to work out what he meant. Then her eyes grew wider as she realised. 'Oh no, Jack, no. You can't be serious!'

'Why not?'

'You just can't!'

'I can. And I am. We'll send them to Paris, we'll get them to talk and, if we're lucky, we might get Dad to come home.'

'I'm grounded,' Lauren said suddenly.

Jack grinned. If Lauren was worrying about how she could leave the house to help, then she couldn't really hate the idea. 'Don't worry, I'll take care of it. How long are you grounded for?'

Lauren shrugged. 'Until my hair goes grey, I think.'

'Well,' Jack grinned, 'I hope you nicked some hair dye as well as a lipstick!'

Lauren howled in anger and threw pillows at his head until Jack decided it was safer to leave.

CHAPTER 28

Jack grinned to himself outside Lauren's room. He leaped down the stairs two at a time.

In the kitchen, Mum was peeling a banana for Billy. 'Well,' she said, looking at Jack, 'at least one of us is happy. It's visiting hours in ten minutes. We're going to the hospital, though we'll be late. Go and tell Lauren that she's coming too and that she's not to go out of my sight.'

Jack noticed that the pink teddy was still on the kitchen table where he'd dropped it. He picked it up and stuffed it into his pocket.

They took the bus as far as the hospital. Billy sat on Mum's lap because the bus was quite full. It was always like that around visiting time, Jack thought. No one really spoke on the journey; Mum was too cross, Lauren was ignoring everyone and Jack just had too much to think about. *If Mum and Dad couldn't get to Paris, then Paris would just have to come to them.*

When they arrived at the hospital, they found Ruby sitting on her bed, dressed in pyjamas. She waved excitedly as soon as she saw them walking towards her room.

'Mummy!' she yelled. 'Mummy, I didn't know if you were coming. You're late. Guess what? I went on the ward today and played with Gracie. She's had all her hair shaved off. Well, some of it anyway. And one of the boys lifted his bandage to show us his stitches. It was gross.'

Mum gave Ruby a hug, holding her close for a long time. 'I'm glad to hear you've been up and about.'

Jack pulled the teddy from his pocket. 'I got you this,' he said.

Ruby stared at it. 'Is it from the machine?' she whispered.

Jack nodded.

Ruby took the teddy as though he were precious and laid him on her lap. 'Thank you,' she said. Then she looked up at him. 'But you shouldn't be spending money!'

Mum laughed. 'Are you giving financial advice, Ruby? Listen, you lot stay quietly in here while I go and talk to the nurses. I'm really glad to see you so much brighter.'

The children were left alone.

'Jack,' Ruby said, 'why are you spending money that should go in the Paris fund? And why are you late? Everyone else's visitors came ages ago.'

Jack looked at Lauren. Would she tell Ruby about the chemist and the lipstick?

Lauren bit her lip. 'I got into a bit of trouble,' she said reluctantly. 'But it's OK now.'

'And the money?' Ruby asked.

Jack grinned. 'We've got enough money. For what I have planned, at least. It came to me in a rush. We don't have to send Mum and Dad all the way to Paris to make friends again. There's an Eiffel Tower right here!'

'Where?' Ruby asked.

'At William's!'

'You're going to make them play adventure golf?' Ruby asked.

Lauren nodded. 'She's only little, but she's talking sense. You'll never get Mum to play golf. Dad maybe, Mum never.'

'Not playing it, no! We turn the Eiffel Tower hole into a fake Paris. We can have a fancy dinner, with wine and candles and a lace tablecloth. Just like in the magazine. We get them to sit opposite each other and

156

serve them a posh meal. If we do it in the evening, they can have the whole place to themselves – all the Wonders of the World right there! If that doesn't calm them down and make them talk to each other, then nothing will.'

Ruby sat still, her legs crossed under her. Her mouth was open but she was smiling slightly. Jack knew that she was picturing the scene in her mind.

'It's a lovely idea,' Ruby whispered finally. 'Will it make Dad come home?'

'Yes,' Jack said.

'No,' Lauren said at the same time. 'But it might get them closure.'

'What's closure?'

Lauren shrugged. 'I'm not sure. But people need it. Shh!' she said suddenly. 'I can hear Mum coming.'

Jack looked out on to the corridor. Mum was just outside with a doctor. They were smiling and nodding at each other. Then Mum came into the room.

'Ruby Tuesday, you're coming home!' Mum said. Her smile was the nicest thing that Jack had seen in days and days.

'When? Now?' Ruby asked.

'No, not now, but in the next couple of days. The doctor says you're on the mend. Isn't that wonderful? We'll have a party for you when you get home.'

Ruby nodded, but she was looking at Jack. He understood. Ruby wanted a party for Mum and Dad much more than she wanted one for herself.

And it was his job to see that they got it.

CHAPTER 29

To: fulldinnerjacket@gmail.com
From: jack.dempsey23@hotmail.co.uk
Subject: Operation Eiffel Tower

Dear Paul,

Operation Eiffel Tower is under way. Objective: get Mum and Dad back together. Actually, that's mine and Ruby's, and probably Billy's objective, though Billy didn't say a lot when we asked him for his objectives. Lauren says our objective should be more realistic. She says we should just concentrate on getting Mum and Dad to speak to each other again. I don't agree.

Tactics: Romance.

Troops will be deployed very soon.

Must rush. Me and Lauren are holding a crisis meeting.

Love,

Jack

CHAPTER 30

Lauren's room became the Headquarters of Operation Eiffel Tower, mostly because she wasn't allowed out of it until Mum decided that her grounding was over.

Jack had found a roll of white wallpaper in the shed and pinned a length of it to Lauren's wall. Lauren scribbled on it in thick black pen, drawing lines and arrows from one word to another, like a spider's web.

'We need equipment,' she said to Jack. 'We need a table and chairs. We need food, a tablecloth, candles, music, wine.' She underlined the words with the tip of her pen as she read them. 'It would be nice to have the River Seine, but William probably wouldn't let us flood the place.'

Jack, who was sitting on the floor, nodded. 'It's like a scavenger hunt. But a really romantic one.' He paused.

160

'Candles are easy. There are some under the sink in case of power cuts. We can just take them.'

Lauren nodded and wrote 'sink' next to 'candles'. 'Food?' she asked. 'I can only do cheese sandwiches or beans on toast.'

'That's not romantic,' Jack said.

'Who do we know who can cook? And not Mum or Dad,' Lauren added quickly.

Jack thought for a moment. Paul was always moaning about Auntie Joyce's cooking, so not her. William? No, he lived off candyfloss and chips from the other stands on the front. Then, he remembered, 'Mrs Khalid! She likes to cook! She cooks for her mum and dad all the time. Perhaps she can help.'

'Good,' Lauren said, adding Mrs Khalid's name to the roll. 'Music? Wine?'

'We can't buy wine, but maybe Mrs Khalid could bring some for Mum and Dad if we explain.'

'Lovely. Tablecloth?'

'How about the Christmas one? It's got pictures of holly on but that doesn't matter and Mum won't notice it's gone missing in the middle of summer.'

'Excellent.' Lauren scribbled another note on the sheet.

'So,' Jack said, 'we just need music. We could take a radio down. Or your CD player.'

161

Lauren wrinkled up her nose in disgust. 'It's not very romantic. There should be a string quartet, or a grand piano.' She sighed. 'But I suppose it will have to do. You'll have to get some batteries from Mrs Khalid so it can work.'

Lauren added the word 'batteries' to the bottom of her list. 'There's a table inside William's hut, isn't there?'

Jack nodded. 'Yes. He plays solitaire on it a lot in winter. In summer, he's too busy so it just gets piled up with stuff. I hope he'll let us do this; I should go and talk to him.'

'Of course he will. You're his championship player!' Lauren grinned. 'I never thought golf would ever come in useful. Especially not crazy golf.'

'Adventure golf,' Jack corrected.

'But *crazy* golf might even get Mum and Dad talking again.'

'That's not my objective,' Jack said. 'I'm doing this so they get back together. There's a chance of that, isn't there?'

Lauren bit her lip.

Jack felt a little shiver of disappointment. She didn't think there was. He knew she didn't.

Lauren shrugged. 'There might be. I don't know. There might.'

CHAPTER 31

'A romantic dinner? Here?' William asked. 'Are you sure?'

Jack looked over at the Eiffel Tower. A family was playing there: a toddler sat on the ground crying, an older girl dripped ice cream from a melting cone on to her club, the mum and dad glared at each other in the heat.

'Only . . .' William said, 'only it's not quite Paris, is it?'

The toddler's sobs turned into screams. His mum snapped something at the man and lifted the toddler into her arms.

'Maybe not,' Jack sighed.

'Still, *Vive la différence,* as they say. Why shouldn't your mum and dad have a nice meal here if that's what they want?'

'Well, I'm not sure it's what *they* want. It's more me and Ruby.'

William nodded. 'Fair enough. But you should get what you want too. When do you want to do it?'

Jack grinned. 'I'm not sure. Soon. When Ruby gets out of hospital.'

'Fine. Just let me know. I can sort you out a table, chairs, some lights too. Maybe a baguette, or a mime artist.' William chuckled to himself.

'Thanks.'

Jack looked at the Eiffel Tower. It was just made of wooden planks, painted with fence paint every autumn. It was about three metres high, with anti-climb paint round the bottom. Could they make it look like the real thing? Would it be enough to get Mum and Dad talking? Would they kiss as the sun set behind the tower?

Yes, Jack thought. *Yes, they would.*

CHAPTER 32

Mrs Khalid clapped her hands together. 'Lamb and garlic potatoes? Or chicken jalfrezi? Or maybe a vegetable tart?'

Jack shrugged.

Mrs Khalid came out from behind the till and wandered up one of the aisles. She picked up a tin, looked at it, then slipped it back into place. 'Ooh, no. Not curry. It should be something French. I don't think I've got any French food though. Fries, maybe? It's not romantic,' she argued with herself, checking out a few more tins. 'I've got it!' she said suddenly. 'Polish! I've got loads of stock, and it's European, close enough to French, no? Pierogi, klopsiki, maybe baranina?'

'Does it taste nice?' Jack asked.

'Of course it tastes nice! I wouldn't cook something nasty. It will be a feast. Fit for a king. I promise.'

'Thank you.'

Mrs Khalid patted Jack's shoulder gently. 'It's nice what you're doing. You're a good boy. I hope it works out for you all.'

Jack looked down at the tiled floor of the shop. 'It will,' he whispered.

CHAPTER 33

Lauren was busy crossing things off on her huge piece of paper – food, candles, tablecloth. Jack nibbled at a sandwich, leaving the crusts on his plate. He put the plate down on the floor.

'You are not leaving that there,' Lauren said.

'But we're still in the middle of planning!'

'I don't care. Take it to the kitchen. I'll get mice in here if you leave crumbs all over the place.'

Jack sighed but picked up the plate and opened Lauren's door.

Mum was in the hallway below.

She was on the phone.

And she was . . . whispering.

Jack stood still. Like statues again, but this time straining to hear what Mum said.

'Fine,' Mum said. 'And he's a divorce lawyer?

Solicitor, then? Good. Day after tomorrow? Is that the soonest? OK. Yes. Ten o'clock. I'll be there.'

She lowered the receiver slowly, then walked towards the kitchen.

Jack realised that his heart was pounding hard, as though he had just run down the stairs and snatched the phone and smashed it down hard. But he hadn't moved.

He stepped back into Lauren's room.

'You've still got that plate,' she said crossly.

'Mum's seeing a divorce lawyer,' Jack whispered.

'When?' Lauren's eyes opened wide.

'Day after tomorrow.'

Lauren paused, then nodded slowly. 'Fine. Then we have to take them to Paris tomorrow. As soon as the crazy golf closes.'

'Adventure golf,' Jack corrected in a voice that didn't sound like his own. He sat down heavily on the bed. A crust slipped off the plate and landed on the carpet. He half-noticed Lauren wince. 'Sorry.' He bent down to pick it up.

'Doesn't matter really,' Lauren said. She came and sat down next to him. 'This doesn't change anything, you know. The objectives stay the same. But now we just have to do it sooner rather than later.'

She put her hand in the middle of Jack's back and

gave him a quick rub, as though she was drying him with a towel. It made him grin, despite himself.

Then he thought of something.

'What about Ruby? We can't do it if she's still in hospital. She'll go mental if we do it without her!'

Lauren stood up and looked at the plan on the wall. 'You're right.' She took the lid off the pen and wrote in big letters: 'Bust Ruby Out Of Hospital Tomorrow'.

'You're joking! We can't do that.'

'Of course we can. The doctor said she's on the mend.'

'Yes, *on the mend*, not actually mended.' Jack thought about burst stitches, about infection, about Ruby's insides suddenly being on the outside in the middle of William's World of Wonders. 'We can't bust her out of hospital.'

Lauren sighed. 'OK, maybe you're right. Let's just go along at visiting hours and find out, shall we?'

'What about the divorce lawyer?'

Lauren grinned. 'Don't worry. This is going to be the most romantic dinner ever seen on a crazy golf course. And it all happens tomorrow.'

She underlined the word 'tomorrow'.

Twice.

CHAPTER 34

Ruby ran towards them when they arrived on the ward. Lauren caught Jack's eye and raised an eyebrow.

'Wait till we hear what the doctor says,' Jack hissed.

Mum scooped Ruby into a hug. 'Hey, sweetheart. Looks like you're feeling better.'

'Gracie and me had a wheelchair race in the corridor and the nurses shouted a bit. Gracie won, but her wheelchair is a proper racing one – I had to borrow a hospital one. Her hair is prickly where it's growing back.'

'Poor Gracie,' Mum said.

Ruby looked a bit confused. 'Why? She won the race. And everyone wants to touch her head where the doctors shaved it.'

'Oh, of course.' Mum grinned.

'Mrs Dempsey?' A nurse stepped out from behind the big desk in the middle of the ward. 'The doctor was hoping for a word with you. As you can see, Ruby's doing much better now and he feels it might be a good idea for her to continue her recuperation at home.' The nurse grinned. 'I think it was the wheelchair race that convinced him.'

'Oh, that's wonderful.' Mum kissed the top of Ruby's head. 'Can she come back with us now?'

'Not now, but I think he said tomorrow. Wait here and I'll page the doctor.'

'Oh, Ruby!' Mum almost squealed. 'I hope you can. I'll come here straight after work to get you.'

Lauren winked at Jack and leaned in to whisper in his ear. 'We'll beat Mum to it. We'll get Ruby and get everyone to William's. Operation Eiffel Tower is go.'

CHAPTER 35

No matter how many times Jack asked, Lauren still wouldn't tell him how she planned on getting Ruby out of the hospital. She just grinned and tapped her nose – *Mind your own business*. Jack went to sleep thinking of the Eiffel Tower and candles and Polish food. He just had to trust that his sister knew what she was doing.

The next morning, Jack felt as though he hadn't slept at all. He was too nervous and excited.

Mum seemed in an odd mood too. 'I called the hospital. They said I can definitely pick Ruby up this evening,' she said, a bit too brightly. 'So I need to get the house shipshape before I go to work.' She swept the breakfast plates away almost before Jack had finished eating. Then she started sweeping the floor.

Lauren glared meaningfully at Jack; she wanted to talk to him upstairs. Jack and Billy followed Lauren out of the kitchen just as Mum was filling a bucket full of soapy water.

'Ruby's getting out of hospital *today*, not tonight,' Lauren said once they'd all got comfortable in her room. 'An hour or two early won't make any difference to the hospital, but Ruby will kill us if she doesn't get to see Mum and Dad at the Eiffel Tower.'

'Good,' Jack said. 'Should I ring Dad, just to make sure he's not doing anything after work?'

'No. It's too suspicious. This has to be a surprise.'

'How is ringing my own dad suspicious?' Jack demanded.

'It just is,' Lauren said. 'Now listen. I'm supposed to be grounded, right?'

'Yes.'

'So you and Billy will have to cover for me while I go out.'

Jack grinned. Espionage. 'OK. When?'

'As soon as I can sneak past Mum.'

'Well, Mum looks like she's going to clean the whole house in time for Ruby getting back. And she's got work later too. We'll just stay in here out of her way and make loads of noise. Mum will think you're play-ing with us. How long will you be?'

'Twenty minutes tops. I'll go as soon as the coast is clear.'

Lauren's chance came when Mum went into the garden with a mountain of wet laundry. 'Right,' she said. 'Make some noise for twenty minutes, but not so much that she comes up to shout. Don't let her know I'm not here.' Lauren scooped up the Paris fund and was gone.

Jack watched Mum peg out the clothes. Even though she worked in a launderette, Jack knew that she preferred the smell of clothes dried outside in the sunshine. She smoothed down a sheet before pegging it neatly. Once the basket was empty and the line was a row of flapping clothes, she turned to come inside.

'Quick, Billy. Tug of war should be a good game. Just don't cry if you lose or Mum might come up.'

They played breathlessly for about half an hour. Then, just as Jack was beginning to get worried, Lauren came in.

'I've been crouching in the front garden for ages, waiting for Mum to move out of view!' she said. 'One of my legs has gone to sleep.'

'Stop moaning,' Jack said. 'Is it all sorted?'

'Yes, of course! Operation Eiffel Tower is all set. We leave at fifteen hundred hours.'

'When?' Jack asked.

Lauren sighed. 'I thought Paul was telling you all about that soldier stuff. We leave as soon as Mum goes to work, OK?'

174

After lunch, Mum gave Lauren another speech. Jack could hear her talking about being responsible, being sensible, being good until Mum got back from work. Then they'd go to the hospital together to fetch Ruby. And Lauren wasn't to get into trouble while Mum was away. Or else.

She was still pretty cross with Lauren.

They waited until they heard the sound of the front door closing.

'Right. I just need to grab some fancy clothes from Mum's wardrobe and then it's time to go and bust Ruby out of hospital!' Lauren said happily.

'Are we getting the bus?' Jack asked.

Lauren grinned. 'Not the bus, no. Come on, I'll show you!'

They went out of the back door. There, in the alley at the end of the garden, was a horse-drawn carriage. Its black exterior shone like new school shoes. The horse was groomed to a similar glossy finish. It wore a plume of red feathers on his head. The driver raised his top hat to them.

'Ta-da!' Lauren said. 'It's one from the front. This is John and Bella. They're going to take us to the hospital, then back, past the B and B to the launderette. All for thirty pounds. I explained why we needed it. John understood.'

The man nodded. 'Yes, my mum and dad split up too, so I'm doing it cheap.'

'But our mum and dad will get back together,' Jack said.

John placed the reins down gently, then hopped down from his seat. Jack could see that his brown eyes, shaded by the hat, were kindly but serious.

'Is that so?' he asked. 'Well, I wouldn't hold my breath if I were you, son. But we all can dream, can't we?'

John lifted Billy up and swung him into the carriage. Billy squealed with joy. A little set of steps folded out from the side of the carriage; Jack and Lauren climbed up. It bounced gently as they all settled in.

John flicked the reins and Bella strode forward. Jack could smell the tang of horse mixed with the warm leather upholstery. It smelled exciting, special. They trotted away from their house, down the road and out on to the front. Billy waved at everyone as they passed. Most people waved back.

Jack rested against the seat. It felt warm on his back, heated by the sun. The sway of the carriage and the steady clop-clop of the horse's hooves made him smile. He shut his eyes.

'Don't go to sleep,' Lauren said. 'There's too much to do. Here's my phone. Ring Mrs Khalid and check she's ready. Then call William, get him to move the table outside. Billy, keep your head inside the carriage.'

Lauren handed over her phone.

Jack stared at it. He had never been allowed to use her phone before. It was sacred. It was precious. Just breathing near it was a life-threatening offence.

'Go on, it won't bite.'

'I don't know the number,' Jack whispered.

'Well, look it up!'

Jack didn't need to be asked twice. He slid his index finger over the screen, selecting options and clicking links. Soon Mrs Khalid was on the line.

'All systems go!' she said.

Then William.

'No time like the present,' he said.

Jack couldn't resist just one look at his emails before he handed the phone back to Lauren. There was a message from Paul:

Good luck with Operation Eiffel Tower. I hope they listen.

Jack cleared the screen then gave back the phone.

The hospital was in view.

'Do you think Ruby's allowed to just walk out?' Lauren asked.

'Maybe.' Jack paused. 'I don't know.'

'Well, only one way to find out. Can you wait for us here, please, John?'

'Righto.' John guided Bella into the car park. She trotted into two empty spaces and stopped – the back of the carriage still stuck out a bit. 'You'd better be quick or they might give me a ticket.' John laughed.

They leaped down from the carriage, Lauren carrying Billy as they raced towards the children's ward.

Ruby was sitting in a wheelchair, trying to make it do wheelies next to the nurse's station. 'Gracie can do wheelies,' she said when she saw them.

'Nice to see you too,' Lauren said. 'Go and put some clothes on – we're taking you home.'

'Cool!' Ruby spun the chair round and sent it racing towards her room.

Pamela, the head nurse, was on duty. 'We're seeing the back of Ruby, then?' she asked with a smile. 'Where's your mum?'

Lauren gave her most grown-up shrug. 'The car park's completely full. There's nowhere to park, so Mum's driving round and round while we come and get Ruby.'

'I thought you came on the bus,' Pamela said.

'Not this time. Dad gave Mum the car today, to get Ruby.' Lauren blushed slightly, but Jack hoped that he was the only one who noticed.

'OK,' Pamela said. 'I know you're a sensible girl. You can tell your mum everything she needs to know. And she can always ring us if she has any questions. The most important thing is that Ruby gets lots of rest . . .'

Jack left Lauren listening to the instructions and went to see where Ruby was. She had pulled on a pair of jeans over her nightie. The pink hem hung down below her T-shirt, but Jack didn't think that mattered. She still looked thin, but she was moving more easily than she had before. She was better. Jack suddenly felt light, as though the soles of his feet weren't touching the ground. He hadn't realised quite how worried he'd been about her until right now.

'Ready?' Jack asked.

Ruby picked up her pink teddy and nodded. 'Ready. I just have to say goodbye.' She raced out of the room and threw her arms round everyone on the ward in turn. She gave the tightest hug to a girl with yellowish skin whose wheelchair had silver and gold hubcaps; that must be Gracie.

'Come on, Ruby,' Lauren said, watching Pamela with a nervous eye.

But Pamela was just watching Ruby. 'She's her own tonic, you know,' she said with a grin. And when it was finally Pamela's turn for a hug, Jack was sure he could see tears glistening in her eyes.

They finally made it out to the car park.

'There's a horse!' Ruby squealed as she saw John.

'And a carriage,' Jack said. 'We're going to pick Mum and Dad up and give them the best night out ever.'

Ruby stopped a metre or so from the horse. 'Is it real?' she whispered.

'It's real,' Lauren said. 'And we're paying by the hour. So hurry up and get in!'

Ruby giggled and climbed up on to the seat.

John swung the carriage round and turned on to the main street. They were going to pick up Dad next.

Lauren ran inside the B and B. while Jack, Billy and Ruby waited in the carriage. Ruby was smiling, but Jack was starting to get butterflies. This had seemed like a good idea. A brilliant idea. But what if Dad refused to come? Or Mum wouldn't speak to Dad? Or worse, what if they both started arguing the same as ever?

Dad came out of the front door. He was in his work clothes: a dusty pair of jeans, a T-shirt and his heavy boots. He was carrying his plastering trowel and there were flecks of plaster on his hands. *Was he doing up the B and B.?* Jack wondered. He frowned. Dad shouldn't be getting too comfortable there.

Lauren came out behind him. She was carrying a shirt and hairbrush, talking to Dad, though Jack was too far away to hear what she was saying. Dad was half-laughing, half-something else. Jack couldn't tell what the other half-something was.

'What are you kids playing at?' Dad asked. 'Ruby!'

he said, seeing her curled up on the seat. 'You're out! You should be resting. What's going on?'

'A surprise,' Lauren said firmly. 'Just get in and put this shirt on. And brush your hair.'

She shoved his shirt at him and pushed him up into the seat. Dad whipped off his T-shirt and pulled on his clean clothes. Suddenly, Jack could smell soap and something else that made up Dad's smell. He wanted to fall into a hug with Dad, but Ruby and Billy had got there first.

'Get off, you two,' Lauren snapped. 'You'll crease the shirt. Dad needs to look nice.'

'Why do I need to look nice?' Dad asked. 'And aren't you meant to be grounded?'

Lauren shrugged. 'Aren't you meant to be putting that shirt on?'

Dad growled something rude about bossy women, but did up the cuffs.

The carriage was moving again, this time heading towards the launderette. Dad stopped talking as he realised what direction they were taking. 'Hey, kids,' he said, 'what's going on? Seriously.'

'A surprise,' Ruby said.

Bella stopped outside the launderette.

This time Lauren prodded Jack. 'I need to do Dad's hair. He never brushes the back. You go and get Mum.

181

Make her wear this dress.' Lauren shoved a plastic bag towards him. He could see red fabric inside.

Jack got down slowly.

Now it was actually happening, he wished that Lauren would do it.

He walked along the pavement and opened the door.

'Jack? Is everything OK? What's wrong?' Mum was leaning on the counter, folding clothes. Auntie Joyce looked over from one of the dryers.

'Everything's fine,' Jack said. 'But you need to put this on and come with me.'

Mum opened the bag. 'What? I can't. What for? Jack, I'm working. I've not got time for games.'

'It isn't a game!' Jack said, louder than he meant to. 'It isn't a game. You have to. Please? Ruby's outside.'

'Ruby?' Mum stood up quickly. 'Why's she out of hospital? Jack, what's going on? Tell me.' Mum's voice sounded worried. She moved towards the door. Jack stood in her way.

'Not until you put the dress on. Mum, it's important.' Mum tried to step around him, but Jack moved into her path. 'I mean it, Mum. Put this on and come with me. You won't regret it.'

'No, but you might,' Mum said grimly. She took the bag and moved quickly toward the back room. Jack heard a rustle as she took the dress out of the bag.

In less than a minute, she was back. She was wearing the dress. It was made from some shiny fabric that shimmered in the late afternoon light. Mum smiled at the look on his face. 'I haven't worn this in ages,' she said, a bit embarrassed. 'It doesn't really fit any more.'

Jack shook his head. 'You look lovely,' he said.

'Oh.' Mum's face flushed a bit pink.

'Come on,' Jack said. 'It's time.'

'Time for what?'

'You'll see. You don't mind, do you, Auntie Joyce?'

Auntie Joyce grinned. 'Lord, no. You look beautiful, Caroline. Go with your boy.'

Outside the launderette, Mum froze. She could see Dad sitting in the carriage. Jack rested his hand gently on Mum's back and eased her forward.

'Jack, what's going on?' she whispered.

Dad's face was stern and silent.

Ruby and Billy had climbed up to sit next to the driver. Lauren was tucked into a corner on the front seat, looking over her shoulder at Mum.

'Oh, God. Ruby,' Mum said. 'Ruby!' She ran forward, her arms outstretched, reaching for Ruby. Mum lifted her down from the driver's side and held her close, her arms wrapped tight around Ruby's back. 'Oh, Ruby.'

'It's OK, Mum. I'm OK,' Ruby said.

'I was going to get you. I was going to bring you home,' Mum said. She lifted her face out of Ruby's shoulder. 'What's she doing out of hospital?' Her voice was thin and fierce. She was looking at Dad.

'It isn't Dad's fault,' Lauren said.

'And you're still grounded! I told you to be sensible! It was the very last thing I said.'

'Mum, I know. Get in, please,' Lauren said.

Mum looked at the carriage, at the empty seat next to Dad. She looked down at Ruby, who smiled up at her. She sighed. 'I don't understand,' she said.

'You will,' Jack replied. 'Come on, get in.'

Mum seemed to be making a decision. Jack held his breath, willing her to agree.

She nodded quickly, then lifted Ruby back up next to the driver.

Billy clapped his hands as Mum climbed into the carriage.

Finally, Jack swung himself up into the space next to Lauren and the ride was under way again.

'Where are we going?' Mum asked.

Dad shrugged; he didn't know either.

'Paris,' Jack said simply.

184

CHAPTER 36

It felt a little bit like being a real family again, Jack thought — all of them riding in the back of a horse-drawn carriage like the tourists did. Except that Mum and Dad sat at opposite ends of their seat, neither of them looking at the other. Dad looked out toward the sea. Mum stared straight ahead, at the back of Ruby's neck. She held herself stiffly, as though she was made of cardboard.

'Nearly there!' Lauren said.

The carriage swung across the road and pulled up outside William's World of Wonders Golf Tour.

'Golf?' Mum barked.

Dad looked confused.

'Paris,' Jack said.

'The Eiffel Tower,' Lauren said. 'Dinner for two in the most romantic place on earth. Come on.'

Jack, Ruby and Billy piled out after Lauren. Dad stepped down. He looked at Mum and then held out his hand to help her down. She ignored it. She sat in the back of the carriage and sighed.

'Lauren, kids,' she said. 'This has gone far enough. Your dad and I have split up. We're not getting back together. We're not having dinner. I want to go back to work right now.'

Jack looked at Mum sitting so rigid in the back of the carriage. He looked at Dad, who was confused and embarrassed. He looked at Ruby and Billy and Lauren – they looked worried. *This wasn't how it was supposed to go.*

'Mum,' Jack said, 'you've had your say. We know what you want. You want a solicitor and a clean break. Dad, you want to see us, but you don't know when or where or how. We *all* know what you two want.

'But do you know what we want?

'Do you?'

Mum bit her lip. Her eyes looked as shiny as the outside of the carriage.

Jack took a deep breath. 'All we want is for you two to talk. You might never be friends again, but you'll always be our mum and our dad and that means you have to talk to each other whether you want to or not. You can't sulk and ignore each other and row whenever

186

it suits you. That is not how it's going to be. Mum, you have to get out of this carriage right now. And you have to eat dinner together, even if you don't want to. You *have* to. Because that's what we want and it's time to listen to us now.'

The last few words stumbled out in a rush. Lauren squeezed the top of his arm, just to tell him that she was there with him. Ruby clapped her hands and even Billy looked pleased.

Mum slowly lowered herself out of the carriage.

She stood in her red dress, with her eyes shining. She held on to the side of the carriage as though it was her support. Then she let go and walked towards them.

It was a short walk to William's World of Wonders. Dad was in front, with Jack and the others in the middle, and Mum came last. Jack checked over his shoulder once or twice, just to make sure that she hadn't turned back. She hadn't. She was right there. He sighed with relief.

The sign on the gate said *Closed*, but it wasn't locked. Inside, the course was deserted. There was just the sound of the water rushing over the Niagara Falls and, further away, the warm whispering of the sea and a busker playing guitar to the last of the tourists on the beach.

Jack peered into William's shed, but he wasn't there. All of his newspapers and junk were on the floor – the table must be by the Eiffel Tower.

Dad looked at Jack, his eyebrows lifted – *What now?*

Jack nodded. 'This way.' He led them down through the Wonders. Each one seemed to shine in the early evening sunlight; the glow from the face of the Sphinx was like a smile encouraging him, the roar of Niagara was like a crowd applauding, the Statue of Liberty seemed to look on in admiration.

And then, there it was.

Paris.

The Eiffel Tower. Dark and mysterious against the pink and orange sky.

A table, laid with a tablecloth and candles, shining cutlery and sparkling glasses.

Two chairs, set close together.

Fairy lights strung in the hedges around the green.

It was like walking into the picture they'd seen in Lauren's magazine.

At the edge of the green Mrs Khalid stood next to William, waiting for them. Jack ran over, his smile as wide as the miniature Grand Canyon. 'Thank you,' he whispered. 'It looks perfect.'

Mrs Khalid nodded. 'William did the lights, I did the table. Not bad, is it? I hope they're hungry. I've got a hot-water bottle in the cool box, keeping everything warm. But they should start soon.'

Mum and Dad stood looking on. They stared at the table and the candles and the lights, but they didn't look at each other.

'Sit down,' Lauren said, pointing at the table.

'Paris, eh?' Dad said uncertainly. He lowered himself into a chair.

Mum sat down next to him, but stared at the empty plate in front of her without saying a word.

Mrs Khalid fussed over the plastic containers in the cool box, pulling out one after another and setting them on the table. 'There you are,' she said. 'Pierogi – dumplings, they're vegetarian – and klopsiki – meat-balls in tomato sauce! Some bread here, for dipping. There's szarlotka for pudding – that's apple pie. Just help yourselves.'

There was a pause. Mum twisted her napkin in her hands.

'Well,' Mrs Khalid said, 'we'll leave you to it. Come on, William; you were going to show me how to get my swing right.'

Mrs Khalid slipped her arm through William's and tugged him away from the green.

The family were left alone.

No one spoke.

Jack heard the angry screech of a seagull somewhere along the beach.

'Did you bring batteries?' Lauren whispered. 'For the CD player?'

'Batteries? Was I supposed to get batteries?'

Lauren clicked her tongue against her teeth. 'No music. There's no music.'

At the table, Mum and Dad seemed frozen.

Lauren shot one last glare at Jack, then walked over to her parents. 'You have to open the lids and put the food on your plates,' she said. 'And when you've done that you have to talk to each other. Pretend you've just met or something.'

Dad reached out and pulled the lid off one of the boxes.

Mum dropped her napkin over her lap.

'Good,' Lauren said. 'We'll be sitting on the wall over there, if you need anything.' She pointed to the wall that marked the edge of the World of Wonders; it dropped down to the beach on the other side.

Jack took Ruby's hand. Lauren picked up Billy and balanced him on her hip. They walked away from the Eiffel Tower, leaving Mum and Dad alone.

They sat down on the wall, facing out to sea. Jack drummed his heels against the rough stones. It was a long drop down on to the sand. He put his arm round Ruby and held her close. Her arm felt thin and he remembered that she had been in a hospital bed just that afternoon. She leaned against him and sighed.

'Are they talking?' Lauren asked.

Jack twisted round and looked back. Mum was holding something white and glistening on the end of her fork. Dad was sipping from his glass.

'It doesn't look like either of them are saying anything,' Jack said. 'Or eating the pierogi.'

'Did Paul say anything about this? About negotiating when no one will talk?' Lauren asked.

Jack thought back over Paul's emails. Had he ever mentioned silence at the negotiating table? 'I don't think so,' Jack said. 'He hasn't been a soldier for very long. He just said that people don't listen when they're angry. That it's too noisy inside their head for them to listen to reason. Are they still too angry, do you think?'

'They're not shouting,' Ruby whispered against his shoulder.

'That's true.'

Lauren glared at the sand and chewed the edge of her fingernail.

'It's romantic enough, isn't it?' Jack asked. 'I mean, it's got everything the picture had, hasn't it?'

'Yes, except for music,' Lauren said scornfully.

'Well,' Jack said, 'even if I had remembered the batteries, the picture in your magazine had a violin player – a real, live person playing romantic music. Not a rubbish CD player.'

Lauren looked at Jack. She was still for a moment, her eyes open wide. Jack wondered if she was going to start a fight with him. Then she grinned. 'Jack, you're a genius. Wait here.'

Lowering herself carefully, she dropped down on to the sand, then raced away as far as the steps with the ice-cream van at the top. There was still a small crowd of people there, enjoying a stroll along the front. They had stopped to listen to the busker.

Jack could just see Lauren talking to the busker, though they were too far away for him to hear what they said.

Then Lauren led the boy down the steps and on to the beach. He held his guitar up, away from the sand, but he followed Lauren.

It was clear that they were arguing the whole way. Eventually, they both stood on the sand below Jack.

'This is Jared,' Lauren said. 'Remember him? He was the one who wouldn't let us be statues on his bit of the front.'

'Hi!' Jack said. Next to him Ruby lifted her hand in a wave, but she was too sleepy to speak.

'Jared is going to go and play for Mum and Dad,' Lauren said.

'Not for free, I'm not,' Jared said hotly.

'You owe us!' Lauren said. 'If you hadn't kicked up such a fuss that day on the beach, we might have raised enough money to send them to the real Paris. And then they might have stayed in love. And not split up. You owe us big time, Jared!'

Jared stood stunned.

'Do you know how to play "Love Me Tender"?' Jack asked.

'Elvis Presley?' Jared sounded dazed. 'I know the tune. It's quite simple, really; it's only got four chords. But I don't know the words.'

'That'll do,' Lauren said grimly. 'It's their song. Dad sang it to Mum at their wedding. Go on over there and play!'

'But –'

'Go!'

Jared sighed. He passed his guitar up to Jack, then scrambled up the wall after it.

'Hey,' Lauren said. 'Help me up.'

Jared reached down and grabbed Lauren's hand, pulling while she jumped, and together he and Jack hoisted her on to the wall.

Jack gave the guitar back to Jared.

'Go,' Lauren said, softly this time.

Jared nodded. He strummed a chord. It sounded clear and strong in the evening air. He plucked a few

193

notes that mixed with the dying sound of the chord. He smiled. 'It's a good song,' he said, winking at Lauren. Lauren's cheeks flushed pink.

Jared turned away.

Jack watched him walk towards Mum and Dad, playing the notes confidently now.

Mum looked up; Jack heard her gasp as she recognised the song.

Dad lowered his glass slowly on to the table.

Jared played a few more bars.

Then Jack noticed that Dad had dropped his head into his hands. His shoulders shook. Was he crying?

Mum reached out and rested her hand over Dad's. Her face shone, candlelight reflecting on tears. She pulled Dad closer.

Beside him, Lauren rested her chin on her knees. She sighed. 'He is nice, isn't he?' she said.

'Who? Dad?'

'No! Jared.'

Jack rolled his eyes.

Then he heard something.

Dad was singing. He was up out of his chair, Mum too. Dad put his arms round her waist and they moved together to the music. He sang the words into Mum's curls.

Then the song came to an end.

There was silence.

Mum and Dad moved apart and sat back down at the table. Mum laughed at something Dad said.

'I think we should go,' Lauren whispered.

'What?' Jack asked. 'But we don't know what's happening. We don't know what they've decided.'

'I know. But I still think we should go. They broke up by themselves; they have to sort it out by themselves. At least we got them talking to each other.'

'But that's not enough!' Jack protested.

Lauren nodded. 'I know, but it will have to do. Come on. Look at Ruby – she's nearly asleep. And Billy. Let's get them back to the carriage. Let's get them home.'

Jack nodded. He lifted Billy and followed Ruby back up through the Wonders, leaving Mum and Dad behind in their own little Paris.

CHAPTER 37

Jack and Lauren put the other two to bed, even though it was only twilight. Then they sat at the kitchen table and waited.

'You're hoping they'll get back together, aren't you?' Lauren said.

Jack shrugged.

'Well, don't.'

'But –'

'Just don't. Don't you remember what it was like? The shouting, the fights, Ruby coming into your room in the middle of the night because she was frightened. Don't you remember hanging around the front in all weathers just because we didn't want to come home and listen to them? Dad calling Mum names? Mum crying and smashing things? You must remember it. You don't want to go back to that, do you?'

Jack shook his head slowly. He didn't want that – whatever he wanted, it wasn't that.

The front door opened.

One set of footsteps.

Mum appeared in the kitchen doorway. She smiled at them both a little sadly. Dad's T-shirt was draped over her bare shoulders, keeping her warm. 'You two still up? That was some stunt you pulled tonight.'

'Operation Eiffel Tower,' Jack whispered.

'What's happening now?' Lauren asked.

'Lauren, you know what's happening. But we did talk. I promise we did. About all of you.'

'Us?' Jack asked.

Mum pulled out a chair and sat down. 'Yes. Me and your dad, we're better off apart. We both know that. But we did it all wrong. You gave a good speech tonight, about us listening to what you want. You were right. We should have all sat down and talked it through. But Dad and I, well, we just weren't up to talking – not then. It would have turned into a row and we didn't want you to see us rowing.'

Jack snorted. He couldn't help himself.

'Oh, sweetheart,' Mum said. 'I'm sorry. We both are. You deserved a proper explanation and you didn't get one. We didn't mean to hurt you, but we did anyway. And we want to make it up to you. But we can't get back together, no matter how much you might want it. We really think that we're all better off this way, you included. But we have come to some decisions. First, Dad is going to move in nearby.'

'Where?' Jack whispered.

'Mrs Khalid says he can rent the flat above her shop. It needs some work, she says, but your dad can fix it up. It's got three bedrooms, so you can go and stay with him. And it's so close, you can pop in any time you want.'

Mum paused and looked at Jack. She reached out and touched his face, just like he'd seen her do with Dad earlier.

'We love you,' Mum said. 'You kids are just amazing. What you did tonight – well . . .' She smiled. 'We're lucky to have you. We're all really lucky.' She stood up. 'I'm going to get changed. It's cold in this dress.' She left the kitchen.

Lauren stood up too. She leaned in and kissed the top of Jack's head. 'It's good,' she said. 'It's all good.'

Jack nodded slowly. It still hurt – it hurt in the middle of his chest. The same pain he'd felt the night

Dad went away. It was still there. But it wasn't so bad; he felt like he could still breathe in spite of it. Perhaps one day it might go completely.

He followed the others upstairs.

He stuck his head into Lauren and Ruby's room. Lauren was taking down their plan from the wall. Jack saw the spidery writing shooting out from the word in the centre – Paris. Then Lauren rolled it up and it was gone.

Ruby had kicked off her duvet. She had her thumb in her mouth and was breathing gently, fast asleep.

'Goodnight,' Jack whispered and went into his own room.

Before he switched off his light, he checked his emails. There was one from Paul:

To: jack.dempsey23@hotmail.co.uk
From: fulldinnerjacket@gmail.com
Subject: RE: Operation Eiffel Tower

Dear Jack,
    How did it go?
    P

Jack typed back quickly:

To: <u>fulldinnerjacket@gmail.com</u>
From: <u>jack.dempsey23@hotmail.co.uk</u>
Subject: RE: Eiffel Tower

Dear Paul,

Dad's going to live on our street, but not in our house. Mum's going to talk to him, but mostly about us. They danced together, but they're not getting back together.

But it's good.

It's all good.

Love,

Jack

MORE FUN-FILLED STORIES BY ELEN CALDECOTT

TALES OF STOLEN ELEPHANTS...

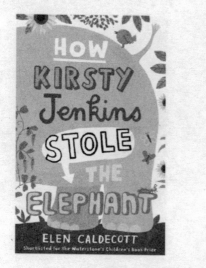

...MYSTERIOUSLY MISSING ANIMALS

MORE FUN-FILLED STORIES BY ELEN CALDECOTT

... COURAGE

... AND ADVENTURE!

'Perfect for Jacqueline Wilson fans'
The Bookseller

WWW.ELENCALDECOTT.COM